Green Eyed Monster

Ivan Romance

Poverty is the state of being extremely poor. When you think of Jamaica, you do not think about poverty. You think about paradise, palm trees, sand, and warm water while dancing. Seeing Jamaican people with happy faces makes you feel at ease, well it's another part of Jamaica.

My name is Eason. A lot of people don't come out alive where I come from. Where I'm from, there is a lot of violence and a lot of pain as I wonder if this is all life has to offer me. I come from the lowest line of Poverty, a place people don't make it where I come from.

Imagine 10 people, living in a fragmented home. The archaic roof is built with old metal with holes in it. When it rains, the water rains on you; the wood is old and worn out by termites.

Rats and roaches were like pets to us because we see them every day when we wake up and hear them when it's time to go to bed. We only had two beds. Some of us had to sleep where the wet spots were, as the rats and roaches would be next to us.

It was so bad that you could catch them lying next to you while roaches would crawl on you. Imagine hand-washing your clothes and underwear with hand soap while wearing the same clothes almost every day. You would have to share your clothes with your brothers and sisters. My clothes looked like rags with dirt Stains on them.

I didn't have any shoes. I had old Sandals, but most of the time, I was barefooted wherever I went.

Imagine missing meals and not being able to drink the best water or eat the best foods. Also, the only time I ate was when I went to school.

I grew up in foster care. My mom had me at a young age and gave birth to me in a public bathroom. When she gave birth, she had left me in the bathroom like I was nothing. A woman found me and turned me into an Orphanage, outside of Kingston. I pretty much had to survive on my own. I pretty much raised myself. I grew up fast and became very mature at a young age.

I've seen killings and drug wars in front of my face. I saw my first dead body at five years old, with a missing head and left arm.

There was a lot of death going on in the poverty around me. A lot of my brothers and sisters from the Orphanage ended up in the streets. A few of them got killed, wanting to be a part of the gang life as some of them had got into prostitution. Few of them got adopted and I've never really kept in touch with any one of them. They were a lot older than me, so they left the Orphanage when they became legal. Of course, the new kids came in the years and I didn't want to get into street life. I just had common sense at a young age and knew it was either death or prison if I went that route.

My dream was to become a professional soccer player. I was pretty good at it, too. I would play soccer, barefooted on the grass and mud. We would pretend that two garbage cans on each side were goalies. One of my teachers from middle school saw me play and told me his brother, who was a coach at the Holy King high school, can use someone like me. I knew it was a Private school. Of course, it costs money to get in, but he told me not to worry. With my skills, I wouldn't have to pay, plus my grades were good enough to get in.

The coach came to watch me play and told me he wanted me to play at the school as I wouldn't have to pay. In exchange for paying money, he wanted me to pay by hard work and keeping my grades up. I told him, "I can do that, sir."

My coach's name was Leroy. He kept asking me to meet my parents, but I had too much pride to tell him how I was living. He followed me home one day and saw my living Situation and wanted to help me with that as well. He talked to my mom as she wouldn't care anyway. In that place, it was Every man for himself anyway. I ended up living with the coach and his wife.

They fed and clothed me like I was their child. His wife, Mrs. Leroy worked at the Room Service at the Kingston Hotel.

She was the best mother I've ever had. She showed me how to cook for myself and clean. Coach knew how to grow food. He owns an acre of land as he would grow fruits and vegetables to sell around the Kingston area in a market called, "Jim's Fresh."

This market would buy wholesales from him and the coach showed me how to grow everything. He even paid me to do it so I can experience my first real job.

It was also a workout; digging holes and carrying crates of corn and watermelon. I even had to pull and carry hay for the horses. We used the soil with the rack equipment. A bail of hay will weigh up to 500 pounds or more. I would have to break it down and carry it. Coach also had iron weights he kept in the horse's barn. He told me to use them so I can become strong enough to lift and pull the bails of hay. Coach became big and strong after years of doing this, so he never used them, but I did. He had a bench press with a curl rack and dumbbells. I work out every day after I finish working. I would do 100 push-ups before I go to bed and 100 push-ups when I woke up.

I just got addicted to working out. Mrs. Leroy fed me pretty well as well; I would eat chicken, beef, eggs, vegetables, rice, and fruits. I was never hungry, but always full.

Coach Leroy and Mrs. Leroy weren't rich, but they gave what they could provide for me. I've felt that I had eaten them out of the house by my last year of high school. I grew to be 6'4 tall, weighing 220 pounds. I was built like an NFL football player, people would tell me.

I also grew long dreadlocks that fall to my upper back. I had smooth dark skin as if my skin and the sun were best friends that hung out every day because working outside every day in

Jamaica heat would do that.

I was also getting attention from girls. They would tell me that they love my green eyes and that I was very handsome and big. It made me feel good. I felt wanted, but I remember when I came into high school, I was only 5'6, weighing only 120 pounds. I was getting healthy and stronger over the years that I gained 100 pounds. I never knew I would grow this tall and big.

The coach was about 5'10 tall. He told me that it was Genetics; maybe my dad was tall. My coach would also warn me about being so big, muscle-wise, it would slow me down, but I was faster; like track star fast.

The coach had me race the 4-time island champion. He won the 100 meters 4 times in a row and I beat him like it was nothing. Coach told me I was Machine and God made me so different that I will do great things and I should have run track doing my off-season, but soccer was my dream, not track and field. I also wanted to party and party all over the island, now that I was making money.

I was able to buy clothes that fit me, thanks to the coach for letting me work with him over the years. I was wearing nice clothing and athletic brands like Nike and Beast Team clothing. I also bought new shoes. My favorite Nikes were these green, yellow and white because of the Jamaican colors.

I also bought new socks, underwear, etc. I looked and felt good. I wasn't rich, but it felt good to have my clothes now without having to share anything. It felt good when my friends and I would walk all over Kingston to talk to women and go to parties.

I would look nice, I also bought myself a cell phone; I got the iPhone 8. I could afford everything because I bought everything off the street from someone, for 100 dollars. I'm sure it was stolen, but I wasn't trying to find out and everything was clean. My phone service came from a Jamaican Phone Company. They gave me unlimited everything for 30 dollars a month. That wasn't a bad price at all, so I thought I was pretty fly in high school. Things were coming along a lot better for me.

The new school that I went to, Holy King Catholic school was different. I had to learn the catholic religion and wear uniforms. The outfit was green polo shirts and tan shorts.

The school was very easy for me, so keeping my grades up was easy. I was very intelligent during my high school years. I got nothing but straight A's that I was the only one in school history to do so. I also took my high school to the island championships four years in a row. We won the 3 out of 4 times we went.

Colleges from the USA offered me a Visa and full Scholarship to come to play for them.

I use to hear how Great America was and the freedom to do what I want; the music and the food look great to eat. I felt like if I move to the USA, I can show my talents and make a lot of money for a better life.

A coach recruiter by the name of Zach Woods from Illinois State University; a fat white man told me that he's been watching me play since my freshman year of High School and loved my speed and ball-handling skills. He also loved my scoring ability alone with my size. I looked like a grown man. I wouldn't have to worry about getting pushed around on the field.

He wanted to offer me a full-ride scholarship and a money grant for living expenses. He felt like I can change the program and I had the grades. I did great on the ACT. To be honest, I just wanted to live the American Dream and travel to play a sport that I love.

It was two other schools that made offers, but I like how Mr. Woods has been watching me for years. He said I will be playing as soon as I step on the field. The other colleges told me that I had to wait a season and I wanted to play soon, so I took the offer and signed to play at the Illinois state university. Mr. Woods saw the conditions of how I was living at coach Leroy's house. The coach wasn't a rich man at all, but it was better how I was living before. Mr. Woods offered that I can move to the college campus early to train and work a job to make money. He said he will have my passport and airplane ticket ready for me.

Once he made that offer, I said yes. Plus I was 18 years old at the time. After I graduated, I wanted to leave. My passport and ticket were handed to me right after I walked the stage. It felt like the best day of my life; to be moving to the USA. Even my teammates were happy for me. I took pictures and left. I got in the car with the coach and his wife. We drove to the airport and I got my bags packed.

We left out the car. It wasn't the best-looking car; it was a white 2001 Ford Escort, but it got us to places. I called Mr. Woods to let him know that I was on my way. My apartment was ready to be moved in.

I thought to myself, " an apartment." I wonder what it looked like. I couldn't wait to see it, but I knew I was going to pay Coach and Mrs. Leroy back and buy them a house and a new car, but we got out of the car and walked into the airport.

I grab my bags and we walked into the airport, it was my first time being inside the airport. It was very nice and clean. I saw White people and other black people that weren't from the island. They looked rich and dressed in very nice clothes. When they walked past me, I heard people speak English, Spanish and other languages. I felt little and poor compared to them, to be honest.

My plane number was called and my coach said, "well, that's your plane; just in time." Coach and his wife told me to be safe and they were proud of me I didn't forget where I came from. I gave them my hugs and told them how thankful I was for them. They were like my parents and I will be forever grateful for them. I started walking on the plane and looked back. They were waving at me. I was nervous. I had never been on a plane before, but I wasn't going to let fear stop anything.

A New Life

CHAPTER 1

When I was on the plane, I sat next to the window. I wanted to see everything. I was sitting next to this pretty black woman; she had long curly hair with green eyes, just like me with light butter skin. She had to be half white or something, plus she Smells very good, very curvy as well. She had to be about 5'4, but her booty and hips were wide. I can tell by just looking at her seat down. She had on a Red and white ISU T-shirt with a red bird in the front. It looked like the college I was going to. I asked her, " excuse me, is that an Illinois State shirt you're wearing?" I asked politely.

She looked at me and said, "Yes it is, I actually graduated there and now I teach accounting there as well, you know someone that goes there?" She asked.

I looked and said, "Well, I'm going there now. This will be my freshman year at the University, small world." I said with a smile.

She looked with a surprised face, "Wow!!! Yes, it is a small world, I can hear your accent. I take it you're from Jamaican yourself, right?" She asked.

I looked and said, "yes, I am from Kingston, my name is Eason. what's your name?"

"My name is Kendra" and we shook hands; looked at each other eyes " Wow you have green eyes, too. I see I never met a dark-skinned brother with green eyes before. It's very different and sexy, to be honest," she said with a voice that kind of turns me on.

"Yes, people from where I'm from tells me that all the time, like Beyoncé said, 'I just woke up like this," I said with a smooth voice with a smile on my face.

"Check you out, quoting the Queen B. I take it you like Beyoncé too, huh?" Kendra asked.

" Yup, I love American music I hope to meet her one day and Jay Z too," I said

" Wow that's dope, I love Reggae music, that's why I came to Jamaica this summer to enjoy the music in person, plus I enjoy the people," Kendra said

"Yes, Reggae is a way of life in Jamaica. It makes you feel good about life; you can go through a bad moment in your life and once you play Reggae, it heals your soul. it can be very therapeutic." I said.

"That's Deep, never thought about it like that before, I see you have the long dreadlocks. Are you a Rasta?"

"No, I am not, haha. I pretty much grew up Catholic. I went to a catholic school as well, I have deep respect for Religion because it saved my life and took me out of a Bad Situation into a good one. I might not be deep in the religion because I'm not a religious person, but I do show respect and I know it is a higher power. you know?" I said

"Yeah, I like that and love how you think. Man, the ladies are going to love you. You're tall and handsome with them big ass muscles, I take it you play football, right? That's why are you coming to America?" Kendra asked with a smile on her face.

"I don't play that type of football. I got a full ride for soccer, soccer is big in Jamaica, same with track and field as well, but soccer is big in Jamaica like how the NBA is big in America." I said.

"Soccer!! Wow, I wouldn't ever guest, but you're right. Soccer is big in Jamaica, we don't have too many brothers on the soccer team. It's a few, but the rest are white boys and a few Mexicans. I hope they don't give you a hard time, they will be dumb if they do."

"Good afternoon, passengers. I am Jessica, the Flight Attendant. This is the pre-boarding announcement for flight 888 to Bloomington IL, we are now inviting those passengers with small children, and any passengers requiring special assistance, to begin boarding at this time. Please have your boarding pass and identification ready. Regular boarding will begin in approximately 5 minutes. Thank you."

"Looks like we getting ready to take off," Kendra said.

"Yeah, not going to lie, this is my first time riding on a plane. I never did this before." I said with a worried voice.

"Don't worry, It's going to be a smooth 8-hour ride," Kendra said in a helpful voice.

"Thanks, I hope so, so tell me more about ISU? Please, it's my first time in America so I'm getting the whole American experience while in college, to be honest" I said.

"Don't worry, I show you around campus and town, we are new friends now. I'll also show you around the best places to eat as well, I know someone your size don't mind eating." Kendra said with a smile on her face.

"I would love that and I'm hungry now I hope they feed us soon. So accounting, I take it that you're good at numbers."

"Yes, I am. A lot of people think accounting is boring, but I love it, plus I can jump into any career, I chose to be a teacher right now. I think it's what I want to get into. How about you? What's your major going to be, have you thought about it yet?" Kendra asked.

"Yes, I'm going to major in business. I already know what I want to do with my life. I'm just using soccer to get to my goals, you know." I said with a confident voice.

"Nice, what's your goals, I mean you don't have to tell me all of them if you don't want to," Kendra asks in a curious voice.

"Well, once I go pro, I'm going to get into the Ganja business, Jamaica is well known for its weed and a lot of places all over the world. I've heard that in some parts of the USA, weed is legal. Eventually, weed will be legal everywhere in the USA in due time. Just mark my words. Weed is the future because the government can make money off of it and will tax it. The world is about making money. Everything is about money, so trust me, it will become legal and I want to be prepared once it does. I'm going to be a big distributor, plus land is cheap in Jamaica. I can buy many acres to grow it, I got other plans as well, but once I get to know you better, I tell you." I said with a smile on my face.

"Well, look at you. A man with a plan. I see that you did your research on it, and trust me, your business will blow up. I believe in you and you're selling a product that sells itself, a product I might use from time to time." Kendra said with a smile on her face.

"I see you must smoke too, huh?" I asked.

"Maybe I do or maybe I don't, but once I get to know you a little better, you will see."

I looked and laughed, I was starting to like Kendra. Our vibe and energy were just right, but I was picturing myself having sex with her as well. Me picking her up in the air, eating her pussy like I haven't eaten in days, picturing me having doggy Style; I need to stop before I get hard. I got on a white shirt too, let me stop.

"Looks like we're starting to move and take off, I see. Let me be smooth and calm." I said.

"This is the best part for me, to be honest. Like a roller coaster, but I'm telling you, it's going to be real smooth."

The plane started speeding up the air road and we started flying up. I looked on my left side out the window and saw how high we were going up as I saw the water while leaving the island. I saw people as we were getting higher and higher, after a while I didn't see the island anymore or any people, just the water. I looked over and Kendra was smiling.

"Good afternoon, passengers. This is your captain speaking. First, I'd like to welcome everyone to Rightwing Flight 888. We are currently cruising at an altitude of 33,000 feet at an airspeed of 400 miles per hour. The time is 1:25 P.M. The weather looks good and with the tailwind on our side, we are expecting to land in Bloomington, IL approximately fifteen minutes ahead of schedule. The weather in Bloomington, IL is clear and sunny, with a high of 80 degrees for this afternoon. If the weather cooperates, we should get a great view of the city as we descend. The cabin crew will come about twenty minutes to offer you a light snack, lunch, and a beverage. The inflight movie will begin shortly after that. I'll talk to you again before we reach our destination. Until then, sit back, relax and enjoy the rest of the flight.

"See it wasn't that bad, now we're up high in the air, passing through the clouds and this nice summer weather," Kendra said in a nice voice.

" You're right. It wasn't that bad, but my ears popped. I learned back in school that when you reach a high altitude, your ears will pop." I said.

"Let me find out you were a good student in high school. Ain't nothing sexier than a black man that's educated." Kendra said.

"Yeah, I might sound like a nerd but I love school. I was the only person in my school history to get straight A's all four years. Funny thing is, I never study. The school work was easy for me. I just read books a lot growing up to kill time before I went to bed as a hobby. My test scores were high, too. If soccer doesn't work out, I know I'll be good anyway"

"Yes, Education is key. I'm trying to tell you but please, once you hit this campus, don't lose focus. The frat parties are going to be a temptation and women are going to be a temptation. You sound like a nice man with a plan with your head on Straight. Don't waste it, please!!! because you're going to go to school with a lot of white kids with money and they are going to judge you. Some will love you, don't get me wrong. It's a lot of caring white people out there, but it's always them that will judge and try to get over you because you ain't from the USA. they going to put Jamaican Stereotypes on you and a lot of Jamaican men Stereotypes about Jamaica men is good, so a lot of white women, not just sisters are going to want a piece of you and that means white men are going to be pissed because not just the fat white women going to want you, the blonde hair cheerleader types as well. You're very good-looking and smart, too. So I'm going to check on you a lot because I care." Kendra said with a caring voice.

"Thank you and trust me, ain't nothing new to the sun. I grew up fast and saw a lot of things, so I'm not just some Jamaican man. I know how it is and I know haters will come and I am prepared to deal with it."

"I hope you're going to deal with it the right way, not by beating them up. At the end of the day, you're still a black man and you're putting your hands on one of the rich kids who will have your ass kicked out of school. Be smart about it. The sad thing about it, I know a few of them will try you, that's why I'm going to talk to one of the coaches for you because I've seen it time after time. White kids get jealous of a black athlete and find a way to get him kicked out of school while he gets to stay in school. Not this time around. I'm not having it. So when it happens, and trust me, it will happen; the coaches will know ahead of time."

I like how Kendra was caring for me and she didn't even know me. I can tell we were going to have a good friendship.

"Thank you very much, but to be honest, that's the last thing on my mind. I can't wait to see college life. So tell me about these frat parties, what's a frat?" I asked.

"You don't know what a fraternity is? Or heard of a fraternity or sorority?" Kendra asks with a surprised face.

"Nope. What is it?" I asked.

" Pretty much a sisterhood or brotherhood people join to network with each other or join to have sisters or brothers they never had. It's a lot of reasons people join. In college joining a sorority wasn't my thing, but I do like the parties, though. Don't be surprised if a frat asks them to join." Kendra said.

"I don't know about that. I'm pretty sure my fraternity is going to be my soccer team, but I am curious. The parties in Jamaica we party day to night talk about the turn-up." I said.

"Haha, I love how you said to turn up. I love your accent, and you have very nice smooth dark chocolate skin, it looks soft. You don't mind if I feel?" Kendra asks.

"Go ahead and touch."

She started rubbing my arms. Her hand felt good and soft. Then she put her hand on my bicep

"Mmmmhmmm you have very nice soft skin too," Kendra said.

"Cocoa butter would do that for you," I said with a smile.

"And you're strong and big. You must have been working out a lot. A lot of the Jamaican men I've seen are lean and cut up, but you're big and cut up. I see like a 50 cent body or something." Kendra said.

"Well, I grew up on a farm, so picking up hay and doing a lot of digging will make you strong, but I did lift weights as well.

Plus my mom cooked. I ate pretty well, but I can move fast" I said.

"Move fast, huh. Well, I'll check out a few of your soccer games, that's for sure. I love your locs as well. You can go to the shop I go to where I get my hair done at" Kendra said.

"Yes, I would love that. You have long hair, too. What's your nationality if you don't mind me asking because of your very light skin." I said.

"My mom is white, that's where I get my green eyes from and my father is black. They met in college. My dad played football at ISU and my mom was a student there. She comes from a small town where there were no black people in Iowa. She grew up on a farm, too. Her parents didn't care who she dated, but other members of the family did. To this day, my mom's family doesn't talk to her. Only just her mom and dad, but she won't give a shit anyway, she said and my dad's people give him jokes and call him OJ, haha. Other than that, they never gave us any problems. My mom worked as a teacher at a high school in Bloomington and my dad is a football coach at the University, so you will see him around campus. He's cool, " Kendra said.

"Sad that you have family members like that. But it didn't break your parent's love for each other. You only have one life and some people are not going to like how you live your life, but hey, it's your life, you know?"

"Right, I like that. So tell me about your mother and father." Kendra said.

I didn't want to tell her about my real parents at all, I just didn't want to talk about it, plus I don't know her like that so I just told her about the coach and Mrs. Leroy.

"My father was my soccer coach and my mother worked at a hotel, but my father will sell fruit in Kingston and also sell fruit to stores, so I was helping him with that," I said.

"Good. That's dope that your father was your coach. I bet he was hard on you because of that and he showed you how to hustle as well, I like that." Kendra said.

"Hey, how are you doing? Would y'all like anything to drink and eat? We are serving steak sandwiches and chicken salads." The Flight Attendant asked with a nice voice.

"I would like a steak sandwich and a cherry Pepsi, please," Kendra said.

"I will have the same thing as her," I said with a smile.

"All right, it will be here within 10 mins." the flight attendant said.

"I see that you're trying to be like me, huh? Haha," Kendra said.

"That steak sandwich sounds pretty good and I've never had a cherry Pepsi before, so why not," I said with a smile on my face.

"I feel ya. I see you have some style. I like your green Jamaica flag snapback. It goes with your Jamaican color Nike's too. white V neck with white shorts. I like it, I see you don't have any tattoos yet" Kendra said.

"No, but that's my plan this summer. I would like both of my arms done, my upper back and chest done." I said.

"That's going to look very nice on you," Kendra said.

We pretty much just talked until our food came and we talked some more. Getting to know each other, she asked things about Jamaica and I asked things about America.

Then after we ate, I fell asleep.

"This is your captain speaking, we made it safe and sound to Bloomington, IL. It is now 8:05 pm. It's a nice, warm night at 70 degrees. Please grab your luggage and thank you. I hope you enjoyed us and had a good night."

I started waking up, I looked and saw Kendra getting up as well.

"Hey, I guess we fell asleep. Well, let's get off this plane. It was nice talking to you. Here, take down my number and text or call me when you make it home safe" Kendra said.

"All right will do, and thanks for the good conversation," I said to her.

I got my bags and got off the plane. I started walking and

looking around, I saw Mr. Woods.

"Hey Eason, over here," Mr. Woods said.

I walked over to him.

"How was the ride over here," Mr. Woods asked.

"It was pretty smooth, I was talking to a professor pretty much the whole time. She works at the university."

"That's great, talk about a small world. But hey, I'm going to take you to your apartment, so you can get some rest. In the morning, I'll see you around campus so you can meet the coaches. You have a roommate as well. He's on the football team. He's staying here for the summer as well. He transferred here from a two-year college, but here, let's go check your apartment out" Mr. Woods said.

I follow Woods. We got to his car. It was a black BMW I8 series. He put my bags in the back for me, it even smells new. I know my cars because I used to read about them and see people around Jamaica drive nice cars around.

"You just got this?" I asked.

"Yup I got it last week, I got a good deal on it."

"Wow!! One day, I'm going to get a car like this." I said.

"You will once you go pro, and I hate to say it, that might be soon. Maybe after this season, but hey, I wouldn't hate you if you go pro after one year. You have the talent. You have what a lot of soccer players wish they had. This Conference is going to hate you, but we are going to love you here. The town is, too."

Mr. Woods said.

"Thanks, that's my dream; to go pro, Travel the world and win the World Cup someday, but my main goal now is to help win a national championship," I said.

"This program never won one of those. We never even came close to winning, to be honest, but maybe this season we can come close. I'll be happy just to go to the playoffs because we haven't been in one in over 30 years, but I'm here to change that. This is my 2nd year here and we will go far this season, I can feel it." Mr. Woods said.

It felt good hearing someone had so much confidence in me to take a program to a national championship that believes I can do it.

"Welp, we are here at the apartments. The name of these apartments is called Indigo apartments. Pretty much a lot of college students at the university live here. It gets wild during the school year. They party hard. You're going to have a lot of fun here, kid. One thing you're going to learn about me is that I'm not one of those asshole coaches that are going to be on your ass. You keep your grades up, come to practice, work hard and play hard during game day, then you should be able to live life and party hard, too. I enjoyed my college years when I played in Arizona, so I'm not going to be the one that says you shouldn't enjoy yourself, because at the end of the day. It's your life, kid. I'm going to tell you the right information, but what you do with that information is up to you." Mr. Woods said.

"Thanks and I will do my best here and also attend a few parties, haha," I said with a smile.

CHAPTER 2

We got out of the car and I got my bags out of the backseat. I followed him and looked around the apartment complex. It looks nice. I had never seen something so nice before. It looks where rich people would live. It was dark, so I couldn't see too much.

"Your apartment is 217 up these stairs. Going up these stairs is going to be somewhat of a leg workout I see, haha. Here; 217. Let me open the door." Mr.Woods said.

We walked into the apartment. It was big and already furnished. It was clean and it smelled nice. I saw a big screen T.V's in the living room. I thought to myself, "I'm going to love this." I remember I am from the slums. I never lived like this before or seen it in person, just on TV.

"Wow, this is nice. I'm going to love it here." I said.

"Yeah, I remember where you came from, so I hope you enjoy it, son. You deserve it." Mr. Woods said in a caring voice.

"But here, let me show you your room so you can get all settled in so I can take you to get something to eat." Mr Woods said.

I looked at my room and I've never had a room like this before. I almost wanted to shed a tear. The bed was big and nice. The room looks like no one had ever lived here before. I walk up to the closet. It looks like I can fit many clothes and shoes in there. Then I saw another door. I opened it, it was a bathroom.

"This is our bathroom?" I asked.

"No, that's your bathroom. No one but yours, I mean, if you have some lady friends that want to use it. gone 'head player, haha. Just kidding, but this is your bathroom."

The bathroom was nice with a marble top sink with a big Mirror. The shower had a glass slide door. There was a walk-in shower.

"I love it!!! I love it!!! I love it!!!" I said, trying to hold back tears.

"Yeah, welcome to being a college athlete. Well, let me get you something to eat." Mr. Woods said.

Ring, ring, ring, "Hold on. it's my wife, let me go talk to her." Mr. Woods said.

I looked around and saw that there were bags next to the bed. It was bed covers and sheets, toothbrushes, toothpaste, and other stuff I needed. I had a big smile on my face.

"Hello? Who is here?" I heard a voice coming out of the living room. So I went to see who it was.

"Hey, you must be my roommate. My name is Trey. I play football here. They said I was going to have a soccer player, not a

Football player as a roommate." Trey said.

"I am a soccer player," I said.

"Damn dawg, you a big ass soccer player, haha," Trey said with a laugh.

I started laughing as well.

"Hey, Eason. Sorry, I have to take care of a few things. I've forgotten I had a few things to do with the wife. This should hold you up for the summer. If you need more, let me know. Hey Trey, can you please take him to get something to eat and show him around a bit?" Mr. Woods asked.

"I got you, coach. He's in good hands." Trey said.

"All right Eason, I will see you tomorrow morning. About 10 am, I'll show you around." Mr Woods said.

"All right, I'll see you then," I said.

Mr. Woods then walked out, but he handed me an envelope. I looked inside and saw nothing but 100 dollar bills, 50 dollar bills, and 20 dollar bills. It was a yellow note inside the envelope. It said, "5,500 dollars." I never had this much money in life. My eyes were wide open.

"I see he gave you some play money as well for the summer," Trey said with a smile.

"Yeah, he did. Just a little bit." I said.

"Yeah, you're a college athlete. You got a full-ride, so they are going to take care of you, money-wise. Better enjoy it, player, I got some money as well. I did one year in a two-year college. I did my thang. Also, I made a name for myself and got a full ride here. I got 3 seasons here." Trey Said.

Trey seems like a cool person. I like his energy. He was a light-skinned brother with deep waves in his head. He had tattoos on his arms, too. He had to be about 6'0 tall and was built like a football player.

"American football isn't played much in Jamaica, but I love to watch the sport," I said.

"I knew you were Jamaican, I can hear the accent pretty good. So what do you want to eat, dawg?" Ivan asked.

"American food, please," I said.

"Bet. I know a good burger joint not that far from here, it doesn't close at all. It's a 24-hour place."

"Yes, let's go there please," I said.

"All right, let's go. You're going to love it. I partied at this campus last year. I was only an hour away from this school, but I'm actually from Chicago, IL. It's about two hours away from here." Ivan said.

"Yeah, I know what Chicago is. I've seen the Bulls play on TV." I said.

"Say what, that's crazy. How do people from different countries watch the NBA? But hey, it's a whole known league, but let's go dawg. I'm hungry myself." Trey said.

We left the apartment, we started walking and talking. I was feeling really good about being here

"So dawg, tell me more about Jamaica. I've never been there but heard stories about it from a TV series. They were promoting the good life of it, but also promoting the poor areas as well like the slums and how the people were living. Sadly, people were wearing the same clothes. Many people, up to 10, live in one home, no power to use, just a very sad situation." Trey said in a carrying voice.

"Yeah, the world loves to promote the paradise vision of Jamaica. It brings a lot of tourists to the island and brings more money in. I've seen many people all over the world." I said.

"Hey dawg, be honest with me bro. Do white women and other women be coming there to have sex with y'all? Haha, be honest. I've been hearing all types of stories about women from Europe and other countries cheating on their husbands and boyfriends, just to get some Island pipe." Ivan said with a laughing voice.

"Haha, to be honest, Yes. I can't lie. I had my share of women. I've slept with white women too, and they gave me money." I said.

"Say whattttt? Damn, they're paying for it like that? Damn. You were in high school smashing shit, huh? Well dawg, you're going to have that lifestyle here too. We both are. Women love athletes. The only beef we might have with is the frat niggas and a few spoiledrich white boys, but other than that, it's going to be smooth here." Ivan said.

"That's good to hear." I said.

"Hey, we're here. Look over there; some females are right there checking you out." Ivan said

I looked, a few girls smiled and waved at me. Looking at me from top to bottom like a piece of meat or something.

"Y'all must be football players?." A random white girl said.

"Yes, I play football and my man just got off the plane from Jamaica. He's actually a soccer player here now."

"Wow, Jamaica. I love Jamaica! I went there a few summers ago. My friends and I had a great time. My name is Lisa by the way. I play softball here." Lisa said with a big smile on her face.

"That's nice. I've seen the sport before on tv. It's just like baseball with a bigger ball, and all the ladies are in great shape as well like yourself." I said.

"Why thank you, handsome. You're in great shape yourself. I never really seen a soccer player as big as you before, you must be really good to come all the way from Jamaica. I'll make sure to check out your games. Here, take my number down. Text me sometimes, handsome. We can hang out." Lisa said.

"That's good to hear." I said.

Lisa was thick with blonde hair. She had blue eyes and

she was very pretty. Not going to lie, I know I was going to hook up in due time the way she kept looking at me.

"Alright, here is my phone, put your phone number in. I'll text you sometime" I said with a smile.

"You better, green eyes." She said as she walked away with her friends.

"Dawg I told you. These girls are going to be all over you. I got her friend's number too, but let's worry about getting something to eat. They have good double bacon cheese burgers. I'm going to get the meal. What do you think you might want?" Trey asked.

I looked at the menu and I just didn't know what to get. It was all American stuff I saw. The only thing I understood was the chicken fries I saw.

"Just give me the same thing you're getting. I haven't had a burger before." I said.

"Say what? Well, we are about to change that ASAP." Trey said.

"Hey, Welcome to King Burger, how may I help you." The cashier said.

"Yes, we would like two double bacon cheeseburgers with everything on it, please. We would like the meals and give us two super lemonades, too. That will be all." Trey said.

"That will be $12.68 please," the cashier said.

"Here, I got $20." Trey said.

"Alright and here is your change. Your order number is 22." The cashier said.

I looked around and saw other college students around. I knew they were college students because they were wearing ISU shirts and they looked around my age. They were sitting down, eating their food. I still couldn't believe I was here. I remember I had to text coach Leroy to let him know that I'm here and made it safe, and I will call him. I texted him that and I texted Kendra, too."

"Hey bro, the food will be ready soon. Let's sit over here and wait." Trey said.

"I owe you for my food, how much was it?" I asked.

"Don't worry about it, it's on me this time. Trust me, they gave me money for the summer as well. I'm about to get more Tatoos and go shopping this summer." Trey said.

"I want some Tatoos as well. I need new clothes too. You don't mind if I come with?" I asked.

"Naw, you can come with. You're my roommate now. We got to look out for each other."

"Order 22 is ready." The cashier said.

"Welp, let me get the food." Trey said.

Beep, I checked my phone and Kendra texted me.

"Hey, you made it to your apartment safely, handsome?" Kendra asked.

"Yes, I did, pretty girl. I'm with my roommate. He's a football player. We are at a place called King Burger" I said.

"Here's the food dawg, you're going to love it. Just watch and their super lemonades are the shit. I got some cheese sauce, too" Trey said

I looked at the food and it looked good. I took a bite of the burger and the fries.

"This is good!! Wow, I can't believe I've been missing out on this." I said.

"I told you dawg, I love to eat good and I know some Jamaican restaurants around here too. If you want to taste it like at home again."

"I have to go there sometime," said.

Beep, I check a text from Kendra.

"Well, I would love to see you tomorrow when you're free. I'm cooking breakfast tomorrow. Maybe I can come by, and pick you up? I'm cooking around 8 am if that's not too early for you?" Kendra said.

"Sure. I'm actually an early bird. Let me get the full address. I know I'm at the indigo apartments."

"You're texting girls already, huh? Don't be surprised if she says she wants you over right now." Ivan said with a smile on his face.

"Yes, it's this girl. She's actually a professor here. We were sitting next to each other on the plane and we were just talking. We had a good convo." I said.

"A professor!!! Wow, that's crazy! What does she look like, and what's her name?" Trey asked,

"She's about 5'4 tall and very thick. Big ass booty and tits. Flat stomach like she workout or something. Long hair too, with green eyes like mine, and she's mixed." I said.

"That sounds like the coach's daughter, Kendra. She's a professor but it's not her, is it?"

I looked and said, "yeah that's her, her name is Kendra." I said.

"Wow!!! How in the hell did you pull that? Boy a lot of my teammates are going to be jealous of you, but I got your back. I won't say anything, I remember her because when I came on a college visit, she was with the coach. He is actually our strength coach and she was fine ass hell." Trey said.

"Yeah she is, we just started talking and had a good convo." I said.

Beep, I got a text from Kendra.

"Funny, I live in those apartments. I live in apartment 315, so it's going to be easy to find me." Kendra texted.

"Well, I'll be there for sure, pretty girl." I said with a smile on my face.

"Dawg, you're about to be the man around this campus. I can see it now. It'll be funny if you get one of her classes. What's your major?" Trey asked.

"Business Management!" I said.

"That's my major as well. Shit, we're going to have some classes together too then. What's your plan when you graduate?" Trey asked.

"To be honest, I'm going pro after this season and I already know what I want to do in life. Play soccer and invest in one of my goals." I said.

"Damn, that's what's up. You must be good ass hell to go pro after one year. I feel you, ain't nothing wrong with that."

"Yeah, that's the plan. What are your plans?" I asked.

"Well, I have 3 more years of football left, but to be honest, going to the NFL isn't my dream. My goal is to own a strip club and I have a clothing brand right now that I've been promoting here on campus. The perfect place to network at."

"A strip club? What are you going to name it? And the clothing brand, what's the name of the brand?" I asked with a smile.

"My strip club name is going to be BBG, a gentleman's club and my brand is called BBG. It stands for 'Big Booty Gang' and I have a lavish brand for men called, "Ivan Davon". Last week, dawg I made 7,500 dollars off my shirts alone. I've been shipping them to different strip clubs all over the nation and having Instagram models promote my brand, too. I've been promoting my brand on Instagram under the name,

'BBG_SelfMade.' People have been going there to order my shirts. Shit, if my sales keep growing like it's been doing and one of these clubs down south team up with me and team up with other clubs for my BBG nights. Shit I will pull you one and done haha. I'm dropping out of college and attacking this full time." Trey said.

"Yeah, you should do it. It sounds like it makes you happy and you're seeing success from it. Might as well do what makes you happy, plus you'll be your own boss and have freedom. One thing I've learned is working for someone will not make you rich." I said.

"Yeah, that's deep and you're right. Soon, one of these clubs will pick me up and make me an offer, giving me a nice contract bonus but till that day comes. I am staying in college, playing football. What else are you trying to get into if you don't mind me asking?" Trey asked.

"Weed. I'm going to buy land where I'm from, grow weed and get into weed distribution." I said.

"Damn, that's a great idea. It will work out for you. So which pro team will you like to play for?" Trey asked.

"I want to be on the Reggae Boyz." I said.

"Reggae Boyz, what's that?" Trey asked.

"It's a Jamaica team. They treat their soccer players like Gods there. Everything's free, plus they get paid great money. They haven't been to the World Cup since 1998, I want to win a

Caribbean Cup with them as well and just want to travel the world." I said with passion in my voice.

"That'll be cool to play for your country. Have they scouted you before?" Trey asked.

"To be honest, I don't know, but that's why I'm here; To make a name for myself so they can hear about me. If they don't hear about me in college, they will when I get drafted to the MLS. America soccer pays well, too. I'll make a name for myself in the league until Jamaica offers me a deal."

"That's great, dawg. I'll check one of your games out, that's for sure. Well, I'm done eating. are you ready to head back?" Trey asked.

"Alright, I am done as well. Let's head back." I said.

We left the King Burger and started walking back home. It was late, about 11pm.

"I'm going to have to workout tomorrow and run two miles to burn this food, haha." I said.

"Yeah, I feel you. I'll show you where the gym is at. I pretty much know where everything is at, I've been here about a month now. I know Mr. Woods want you to meet the other coaches you have. After that, we hit the gym. I'm going to workout myself." Trey said.

"Cool, I would like that." I said.

Beep, I got a text from Kendra.

"Do you have an Instagram so I can follow you, maybe

look at your pictures?" Kendra texted with a smile.

I actually made an IG page last month. I wasn't into social media like that; I've had 5 pictures of myself on there and some shirtless pictures.

"Yes, I do. My IG Page is GreenEye_Monster." I texted Kendra.

"Oh yeah, I also want to go shopping tomorrow too, If you don't mind showing me the mall. I want to buy that shirt you're wearing too." I said to Trey.

"Yeah the mall is actually not that far. I have a Jeep so I got you. You wear a size XL I take it, right?" Trey asked.

"Yes, I am. Do the stores have it in yellow or green? They are my favorite colors." I asked.

"I'm pretty sure they do. I'll show you the best shopping stores." Trey said.

We made it to our apartment and I just wanted to shower and sleep.

"Hey dawg, I'm going to bed. I'll see you tomorrow." Trey said.

"Alright." I said.

Beep, I got a text from Kendra.

"Wow, you look great. You have a very nice body and your smile is perfect. I see that you have nice white teeth and I see you have a deep 6 pack. I liked all 5 of your photos. you need more pictures, that's for sure. I'm going to nickname you, 'Rude Boy.' I just like the sound of it and follow me back. Show me some love as well." Kendra texted.

I walked in my room and looked at her IG Page. She looks great, she even had photos of her in a swimsuit. I was getting hard just by looking at her photos. I knew for a fact when I got in the shower, I was going to imagine myself having sex with her and jack off.

I looked around my room and started unpacking. I put my shoes in the closet and saw hangers. I hung my clothes up, made my bed up with the new sheets and covers. I had some big pillows, too. The room was clean and it smelled good. I also had some Jamaican posters I wanted to hang up, but I would get to it later. I got my under clothes ready. I saw I had some Irish spring soap, they also got me some deodorant and also some dry towels. I saw two big beis, too. I guess I can put my dirty clothes in.

I took my clothes off, too. I got naked and put my underwear in the clothes bin. I wanted to keep my room clean, that's for sure. I never lived in such a nice place. I didn't see any mice or bugs at all. I walked into the bathroom, turned the shower on and got in. I took the soap and started washing my body, closed my eyes and started thinking of Kendra in the photos I saw and started jacking off. I pictured myself having sex with Kendra.

In my imagination while in the shower, Kendra just

walked in with no clothes on. She came in the shower, then she started kissing all over my abs and started jacking me off. I picked her up and sat her on my dick and started giving her strokes while water was coming down her body. I just imagined how warm and good her pussy felt. Her moaning rude boy in my ears. Then I came all over the shower floor and opened my eyes.

I finished my shower and took a towel to dry my body off. I went to brush my teeth and wash my mouth out with the green mouthwash I saw as well. I saw that my phone had a text, so I walked over to check it out. It was from Kendra saying, goodnight and see you in the morning. So I texted her back and said goodnight as well.

I got in bed and lay down, thinking about life and my goals and thinking that I was thankful to be here. I was laying in a bed that was clean and felt so comfortable. I saw the remote next to the bed on a night stand, so I put my phone on a charger. It was an iPhone changer already, so I used that and put my alarm on at 7:30 am. I turned to the soccer channel. I saw that they were just talking about the top soccer teams in the MLS. I then fell asleep.

Beep, beep, beep. I woke up. It was 7:30am. I saw that the sunlight was shining through my window. The TV was still on.

I went to do 100 push ups knocked them out. Then, I brushed my teeth and put on my workout clothes. I put on a white T-shirt with the Jamaica flag on it. Put on some gym shorts, green and yellow Nike workout shoes. I grabbed my phone and texted Kendra good morning and I'll be upstairs to her place soon.

I went to the living room and the kitchen. I started hearing moaning and smacking coming from Trey's room. The bed was shaking. I got close to the door to be nosey and heard, "Yes Trey yesss, please don't stop!" and I heard him said, "I told your big booty ass I was going to hit this one day, talking all that shit and can't even take dick, stop running." I heard another smack like he was smacking her ass.

I backed away and let him finish what he was doing. Sounded like he was giving it to her. I hope I can get some pretty soon, too. I haven't had sex in about two weeks now, it was from a older woman and, visiting the island. She was 35 years old. It was her birthday present. She was from Houston, TX and gave me her number.

My phone started ringing and it was Coach Leroy. I picked up: "Hello coach, how are you doing?" I asked with a smile on my face.

"So you made it safe to America, I see. My wife and I are very happy for you. People are starting to talk about you around here. They can't wait to see you play." Coach Leroy said.

"Yes, I'm very excited. I'm meeting the coaches today."

"Good, well I'm not going to keep you on the phone, I have to get ready for work. Just keep me updated and we are proud of you. Here, Mrs Leroy wants to talk to you."

"Hey, how are you doing, Eason? I just wanted to say we are watching you, even though we are not there in person. We are there in spirit and God has blessed you with talents to see the world to do big things. We are blessed to be a part of your journey." Mrs Leroy said.

"Thank you and I love you very much." I said.

"We love you too, have a good day now. Talk to you later, bye."

I felt proud and happy to have people that care for me. My foster mom she wasn't caring like my Mrs Leroy, but she's wasn't the worst either. She had 10 other kids to watch and take care of and at a young age, I knew that, but time yo time, I wonder about my real mom and what she looks like. Do she ever think of me? But one day, maybe, just one day I will get to meet her.

Beep, I got a text from Kendra.

"Breakfast is done. You can come up now, handsome," Kendra texted me with a smile.

So, I left the apartment and went upstairs to her apartment 315, then I knocked on the door. She then came to open the door.

She came to the door wearing a white tank top and pink basketball shorts with pink socks on with her hair tied up. She gave me a hug, I embraced her and gave her a tight strong hug like I didn't want to let go.

"That was a nice hug, plus you feel good. Well, come in." Kendra said.

I watched her ass go up and down. I told myself to stop looking so I won't get hard, but then I saw pack boxes too like she was moving.

"It smells good. I see you made pancakes, eggs and bacon. It also looks good. Also are you moving?" I asked.

"Yes. I pretty much was living here during my college years here and still have a roommate. I'm older now and grew out of it. During the school year, it gets loud around here. I got an apartment off campus. A one bedroom and it's a pretty chill place, but you're going to have fun all summer. It's some stuff to do, even though it's only May. School doesn't start till August 15th. You'll find something to do. If you are looking for a part time job, my friend is hiring a personal trainer and you pretty much just be training women. You're in good shape and you look good, I'm pretty sure you'll get a ton of business. There will be some money coming in, you know."

"I'm down to do it. Where is the gym at and what's the name of it?" I asked.

"You can start eating first. I want to know if you like the food, handsome." Kendra said.

I started eating and the food was pretty good. I ate my food and looked deep in her eyes at the same time. I wanted Kendra. I started to crave her. I wanted her body more and more.

I want her lips against mine and her skin rubbing against mine. I then pour syrup on the pancakes.

"This is good. I see you're a good cook." I said.

"Thank you. I try to be, but the name of the gym is called, 'Your Fitnesses.' I'll make sure to tell her you are looking for a job. Her name is Jasmine. She goes to the university as well." Kendra said.

"Thank you, and thank you for the food, too. You've been so nice to me." I said.

"Anytime. So who is your roommate? Y'all went out to eat last night?" Kendra asked.

"Yes, we went to King Burger and my roommate's name is Trey. He plays football here." I said.

"Trey. You're talking about that light skinned brother that just transferred here?" Kendra asked.

"Yes. He came from another college, he said." I told Kendra.

"Yeah, I saw him around. He's going to play linebacker here and few of my friends have a crush on him. I think one of my friends is over there now actually. She texted me this morning, saying she was going over." Kendra said.

"Yeah, I think I heard her if you get what I mean." I said with a smile.

"Yeah, I knew she went over there to do the nasty. He's alright, but I love my men to be chocolate and handsome."

Kendra said with a flirty voice.

"Well, chocolate is good for you." I said. Then I started looking into her eyes and I started thinking and wondering if she tasted like these pancakes I was eating. I would lick her plate and a lot more if she let me. I space out into her eyes, thinking about what I wanted to do with her. Then she looked into my eyes.

"Yes it is, women love chocolate. You got some syrup on your chin." Kendra said.

I try to get it off.

"Did it come off?" I asked.

"Nope, I'll get it." she said.

Then she walked over and licked her finger to wipe it off. I got hard right then and there. I just looked at her and couldn't move. I wanted her body even more.

"Damn, you got more on your lip. I'll get that off, too" Kendra said.

She then licked it off my lip real slow with her tongue. My dick got super hard. I knew if I got out of my chair, she would see it.

"There, it's gone. I licked it off you." Kendra said, giving me bedroom eyes.

We looked at each other like we were reading each other's mind. I felt like she was reading my thoughts of what I wanted to do to her. She then grabbed my face with her soft hand.

We both started kissing. I started grabbing her ass like it was mine.

Squeezing it as I started kissing and licking her neck. She then started moaning.

"Yes, Eason. Just right there. I love being kissed on my neck, mmmmm." Kendra moans.

I stood up and she saw how hard I was by the look in her eyes. She wasn't disappointed.

"Wow, I wanna see it up close. That's a very nice dick print." Kendra said.

She started pulling my shorts down and my dick was by her face. Then, she started licking my dick as I started moaning a little bit. I put my hand on her head and she started sucking it real slow. All I saw was my 9inch dick being sucked and she massaged my balls, too. She took my dick out her mouth.

"Damn you have a big dick, rude boy." She said with a smile. Boy, y'all Jamaican men be packing here. Let's go to my room right quick." Kendra said. She started pulling my arm into her room.

I checked to see what time it was. It was 9:10 am. Alright, but I do have to meet the coaches at 10am.

"Don't worry, rude boy. It's just a quickie. Don't worry."

We walked into her room and she then closed the door. Her room basically looked like mine, but with a woman's style to it. She walked over to the dresser and gave me a Magnum thin style condom.

"Here, I'll put it on for you, rude boy." Kendra said.

She started kissing and licking my abs while rolling the condom on my dick. I wanted this so bad.

"Lay down on the edge of the bed, I'm about to ride you. You got five mins to cum, rude boy." Kendra said in a sexy voice.

I laid down and then she sat her big booty on dick in a *reverse cowgirl position*. As she slid in, I felt how warm and wet she was. Her pussy felt like warm Jamaica water.

She looked back at me and started to moan.

"Yes, Eason, just like that. Nice and slow. I want to feel all of you." Kendra said, while riding my dick and her eyes being close.

I grabbed her tiny waist and started giving her faster strokes. She moaned louder, trying to hold her moaning in. I started saying shit in each stroke I gave her, and I started going faster. Her ass started clapping and her ass was swallowing my dick like it was nothing.

"Yes, rude boy! Damn, you have some good ass dick. Keep going, please keep going." Kendra moaned.

I moaned some, too. My dreads started getting in my face. I picked her up and started giving her backshots, doggy style.

"Damn, you feel so good, Kendra!!!" I said.

'I'm about to cum!!' Rude boy please go faster" Kendra moaned.

The bed started shaking and her big booty started clapping on my dick. I then started going faster.

"Yes, I'm cumming!!!" Kendra said, Then she started screaming and grabbing her pillow to scream and moan more. She screamed inside the pillow. I can feel her pussy tapping out. She came as I watched her hands pull the sheets.

Her moaning and ass shaking got to me.

I couldn't hold my nut any longer "I'm about to cum as well!" I said, so I went faster and faster. Then the bed started moving like I was pushing it and the headboard started smacking the wall.

"I'm cumming, too Kendra!" I moaned.

"Yes, rude boy, hurry up now." Kendra said while looking at me and her big booty. Then, she smiled at me.

I moaned and started cumming hard! " Yes, here it comes!!!" I moaned.

"Yes, rude boy. Come hard for me right now. Don't hold back at all" she said.

"Yes, yes, here it comes! Mmmhmmm mmmhmmm mhmmmm!"

I came hard. I needed it. I felt relaxed. I can see she was relaxed as well. I pulled out and saw that the condom was full of my nuts and my balls were wet from her pussy.

I also smiled at her. She smiled at me back while we were trying to catch our breath. I asked her if I could use her bathroom to clean up. She got up and gave me a hand towel. I went inside the bathroom, flushed the condom and I took some soap and water to clean my dick and balls. She took the towel and put it in her dirty towel bend.

"Wow rude boy, that was good. I couldn't help myself. We're going to have to hook up again, that's for sure." Kendra said with a smile.

"Yes, I agree. Thank you for feeding me and sharing your body with me." I said.

"Trust me, I'll be sharing it with you more, but you have to get ready to meet your coaches. It's 9:25 am. I'll walk you to the door." Kendra said.

I came out of the room then I saw a girl in the kitchen. It was a Latina girl.

"Hey, I was asleep then y'all woke me up, girl." The latina girl said.

She was thick as well with long dark hair, pretty brown eyes and a very nice smile. She had to be about 5'8. She also had tan skin.

"My bad girl, for some reason, I thought you were gone. I feel embarrassed." Kendra said.

"It's cool, we're grown. Who is this tall football player you were getting busy with?" The latina girl asked.

"His name is Eason. This is the Jamaican I was telling you about, who I met on the plane. Eason, this is Kayla." Kendra said.

"I get it, that's why she was calling you Rude Boy, haha." Kayla said.

"I'm speechless, this is awkward, but I have to get ready to go. It was nice meeting you, Kayla. I'll talk to you later, Kendra." I said as she gave me a hug.

I went downstairs to my apartment and I saw Trey seating in the living room, watching T.V.

"Hey what's up dawg, what are you up to this morning?" Trey asked.

"Not much, just went for a walk." I said.

I never kiss and tell. I had nothing to prove to anyone about my sex life and I respect the women I sleep with. If the woman tells, then that's their business, but I will never talk about it.

"Yeah, not much out there. A lot of people packed up and left already. We can hit the bars later tonight and see what's out there. People from this town go out."

"Yeah, I'm down for that and I still would like to go shopping today as well." I said.

Ring, ring, ring. I pick up the phone. It was Mr. Woods.

"Hey, just calling to remind you about meeting the coaches. I'm actually down stairs in the car waiting." Mr Woods said.

"Yes, I'm ready. I'll be down there right now." I said.

"Alright. See you when you get here." Mr Woods said, then he hung up.

"Welp, I'm meeting the coaches. I'll see you later. Get a workout in before we hit the mall." I said.

"Yup, I'm down for that. I'm actually going to meet you at the athletic office where you will be meeting your coaches at. The gym is actually in the same building." Trey said.

"Cool, talk to you later. Let me get your number." I asked.

After I got Trey's number, I went downstairs and saw Mr. Woods in the car. I got inside as he drove off.

"Nice shirt. I need a Jamaican shirt myself. They have a talented team." Mr. Woods said.

"Yeah, one day, I'm going to play for them. That will be a dream come true." I said.

"It can happen, that's for sure. So this is the head coach, coach Brown. This is his first year. The last coach got fired, so he's new. They actually have a lot of new coaching staffs. They got tired of losing so these coaches are just as new as you've seen them in your film. They love you." Mr. Woods said.

"Wow, that's a good thing to hear. Well, I hope they like me." I said.

"Welp, we're here. Let's go meet them." Mr. Woods said.

We got out of the car. The building was nice and I could see the soccer field, too. I saw the school logo with a red bird in the middle of the field. We walked inside. It was nice and big inside the building. I saw trophies in the glass cases and pictures of athletes. Basketball players, football players and baseball players. We kept walking down the hall and I saw soccer players in team photos, trophies from the 1980s and a conference trophy from 1995. That's all I saw, then we made it to the office.

I saw other students in the office. Then, I saw two grown white men in the office, wearing ISU Polo's that said, "ISU soccer" Mr. Woods and I walked in.

"Hey, coach Brown and coach Smith, this is Eason." Mr, Woods said.

"It's a pleasure to meet you Eason, I'm coach Brown. The new head coach. I love your film. You have a lot of talent. I'm happy you joined our program." Coach Brown said, after shaking my hand.

"It's nice to meet you, coach. I'm happy to be here as well."

"I am coach Smith. I'm the Assistant Coach. I am new to this program as well but, son.

You looked like a football player, to be honest. You're tall and a big dude. I saw your film and couldn't believe how fast you were and saw your ball handling skills. I never seen it before, to be honest, but hey, good thing you're playing for us." Coach Smith said with a smile.

"Yes, I grew up on a farm, ate pretty well and worked out as well. But, I'm actually only 210 pounds." I said.

"Wow!! You have a lot of lean muscle on you. I mean, I can see your 6 pack through your shirt, so I believe you, haha." Coach Brown said with a smile.

"Oh yeah, this is Josh. He's a senior this season. If he has another good season, it's a high chance he's going pro after the season." Mr. Woods said.

"That's the plan, coach, but I have to get ready to go. It was nice meeting you, Eason. I'll see you around."

"You too." I said.

"Oh yeah. Well, we're not going to keep you long, Eason. We just wanted to meet you. Practice doesn't start until August 1st, so you got a lot of time this summer to enjoy yourself. Here is my card if you need anything. I'm about to enjoy my summer as well, haha." Coach Brown said as he left.

"Yes also, here is your ISU soccer book bag with some shirts and shorts in there. We got your size from Mr. Woods. Size XL, right?" Coach Smith asked.

"Yes sir, that's my size." I said with a smile on my face.

"Good, well I'll see you when camp start, so stay healthy, plus you got coach Woods here, too. He is our Strength coach. I am pretty sure He's going to be checking on you to make sure you're healthy as well." coach Smith said.

"Yes, I'm watching you like a hawk, Eason. Haha." Coach

Woods said.

"Trust me, I love working out, so you don't have to worry about me. I'm actually meeting Trey to workout. I think that's him outside the office waiting." I said.

"Well, good. We won't stop you. We'll talk to you later." coach Woods said.

"Alright, talk to you later, coaches."

I walked outside the office to talk to Trey.

"I see they gave you some 'Welcome To ISU' gifts. That's a nice book bag as well." Trey said.

"Yeah, it looked like they gave me like five T-shirts too, with a few workout shorts. So where is the gym?" I asked.

"It's this way down the hall. I'm working on my upper body today. I know some of my teammates might be in there as well. I saw some walking to the gym." Trey said.

"Well, that's cool. I want to see what the gym looks like." I said.

We walked to the gym, and it was big as I saw people working out. It also had a track upstairs and I saw a basketball court too. I also saw people playing basketball.

"Hey Eason, how are you doing?"

I looked and it was Lisa, the white girl from last night from King Burger. She gave me a hug.

"Hey Lisa, we're just here to workout." I said.

"Well, don't forget to text me, handsome so we can hang

out." Lisa said with a smile.

"I won't forget." I said.

Then she walked off.

"Damn Dawg, she's on you bro. She wants you to hit ASAP I see, haha. But

Hey, let's use that bench press over there. I like to warm up with 135." Trey said.

We walked over to the bench press and put 135 pounds on the bench. It was iron plates, just how I like it and what I used back at home.

"Alright, I'm about to knock out 10 first." Trey said.

I saw some big guys looking at us. I'm pretty sure they were football players and they started walking towards us. There were 3 of them. Two of them were white and the other was black. After Trey did 10 reps, I lay down and did my ten reps as well.

"Let's put 225 on there. I'm going to burn out to see how much I can do." Trey said.

"Alright, I'm down for that, too. I never tried to see how much I can do." I said.

So we put 225 pounds on the bench press.

"Alright, count for me please." Trey asked.

So I counted for Trey. He did 225, 24 times.

"That was good, you have good strength and endurance." I said.

"Thanks, my goal is to do 30 by the end of the year. Alright, your turn. I know I can get 20 out of you." Trey said.

"You don't mind if I knock in a few with you guys? I'm Jordan by the way. I played the O line here." Jordan asked.

Jordan was a big guy. He had to be about 6'5, 320 pounds. He was a white guy, too.

"Naw go ahead, get you some." Trey said.

Jordan then lay on the bench and started doing 225 and he got past 25.

Trey then whispered to me, "He's going over here because all the hoes are looking at us. He is trying to show us he's stronger than us. He plays O line and you're 300 pounds. You better be stronger than us, fat motherfucker" Trey said.

I laughed a little bit when he said that. I looked and girls were watching us.

Jordan then stopped at 32 reps.

"Thanks, I just wanted to knock that out of the way." Jordan said.

"Alright, my turn. I'm about to knock some of these out as well." I said.

"Just don't go past 32, haha. That's the school record and I am the record holder. Just playing, I don't expect you to do that much." Jordan said in a sarcastic way.

"Alright big dawg, we see that you're strong. It's my man's Eason turn. He is about to knock a few of these out himself." Trey said.

"Naw, he might get 15 at the most." Jordan said.

"Just 15? No way, he's that strong" Trey said.

"He looked strong, but let's see if he's strong."

"Bet. Show them you got this." Trey said.

"I didn't come to workout for competition. I came to workout, to workout. I don't want to make you look bad, so you can't be mad at me." I said.

I looked around and girls started to look. I saw Josh, my new teammate, watching too.

"I knew he couldn't do it, talking about looking bad. You just can't do it." Jordan said.

"Ok, I'll do it, but I'm about to hurt your feelings and don't get mad if I do." I said.

So I laid on the bench press and started lifting 225. I started fast and got past 10. Then I passed 15.

"I told you. My boy is strong. Keep going, Eason." Trey said.

I kept going. I got to 20 then to 25.

"Damn, you got more than me Trey said."

I kept going. I got pass 28, then I got pass 32.

"Damn, he just broke your record!!!!! Keep going, Eason."

I kept going, then I got pass 37, then I got pass 42.

"Damn, keep going." Trey said.

I kept going, then I passed 42. I stopped at 48 reps.

"Yeah!!!!!!! Dawg!!!! Damn, you're strong ass shit!!!! 48 times, I have never seen that done before in person!" Trey said after giving me a handshake.

"I just saw that, son. I work here in the gym. I'll make sure to put you in the record book. Wow. 48 times. You're now the gym holder. I am pretty sure you're the conference holder as well. Great job. Your name is Eason, right?" The gym guy asked.

"Yes, that's my name," I said.

"Yeah, yeah, yeah, but let's see how strong you really are. Put 315 on the bench press." Jordan said.

"Dawg, you're doing the most. You're just mad he killed your record." Trey said.

"I don't care about that record. I'm the strongest overall in this conference. Put 315 pounds on the bench press, please."

"That's a lot of weight, dawg. If you can't lift that, trust me, I understand. Soccer players don't lift heavy.

Plus I just put two and two together, this nigga must like Lisa. That white girl that likes you and shit, so he's trying to show off in front of you because I saw them talking when I was waiting on you." Trey said.

"It's fine, I can do it." I said.

So we put 315 pounds on the bench press. We put 3 plates on each side and hear the plates smash against each other. Jordan then laid down on the bench and did 315 pounds, 10 times.

"Your turn." Jordan said.

So I got under the bench press, picked up the weight and did it up to 15 times.

"Damn!!!!!! Dawg 315 for 15 times. I can only hit that shit two times." Trey said with a surprised look.

"That's it, I'm about to end this right now. Put 515 on the bench press, big boy weight." Jordan said.

We put 515 on the bench press.

"Help me lift it off, y'all." Jordan asked his teammates.

Jordan then laid on the bench press.

"Alright. 1, 2, 3, lift off." Jordan said.

He got help to take the bar off the rack and, he then pressed 515 pounds. He put it on his chest and slowly lifted it off, but he pressed 515 people. Came around and started clapping.

"Damn, this nigga is strong. They must feed him whole cows, growing up. You proved that you're strong, anyway." Trey said.

"Put 550 pounds on the bench press, please"

"No fucking way you're hitting 550 pounds. You're going to hurt yourself. You're crazy." Jordan said.

"Please put 550 pounds on the bench press." I said with a serious voice.

"Damn, that's a lot of weight. That kind of weight can hurt you, but if you think you can do it, go 'head" Trey said.

His teammates put 550 pounds on me. The bench bar was

bending because there was so much weight on it.

I got under the bench press and put my arms on the bench bar.

I gotta see this. More people came around and I saw people recording with their phones. I just remembered my Mrs. Leroy's voice, saying "you're going to be great and do amazing things to the world." I closed my eyes then I opened them.

I took the weight off the bar and put the weight on my chest. I lifted it off my chest and put it on the bar. The sound of it slammed! I got up and saw people hand clapping and saw Trey, jumping up and down with a big smile on his voice.

"Ladies and gentlemen, we have the school and conference history bench holder. No one in the school's history has ever bench pressed 550 pounds. The record belongs to Eason.." The gym guy said.

I looked, people kept clapping and cheering for me. It felt amazing.

"Dawg, you're strong as fuck, man. Got damn, what were they feeding you in Jamaica!!!" Trey said with a big smile on his face.

"Steroids!!!! Ain't no way he's that strong, naturally. They were feeding him steroids." Jordan said with a hateful voice.

"Shut the fuck up. Ain't no one on no steroids. You're just mad he weighs less than you and he's stronger than you."

"I've never done such a thing in my life. I'll do a drug test for you right now." I said.

"You don't have to explain shit to him." Trey said.

"Whatever. I'm out of here." Jordan said.

"Damn, you're strong. You play DE for us? I'm Kyle, by the way." Kyle said.

"No, I'm a soccer player. I moved here from Jamaica." I said.

"Wow, how strong are you? You're playing the wrong football I would say, haha." Kyle said.

"Man, I'm saying, dawg." Trey said.

"What about you? You're playing, right?" Kyle asked Trey.

"Yes. I transferred here. This will be my sophomore season, I play middle linebacker." Trey said.

"Yeah, I heard about you. Your name is Trey Jones. You were doing your thing. You had 110 Tackles with 15 sacks. You also got 7 Interceptions, 6 of them were touchdowns. I'm Jackson. I'm the right side linebacker. This is my last season."

"Yeah, I try to be alright." Trey said in a humbled way.

"We both are seniors this year. Sounds like you can ball. Can't wait to play with you, but it was nice knowing y'all. I'm doing summer classes, and don't worry about Jordan. He was just hating because Lisa was talking to you." Jackson said.

Trey then looked at me and said, "I told you, dawg."

"We see y'all around campus. We live at indigo apartments. We have kick backs. Come over sometime. We are having girls over and if you smoke, we got it if you. Drinks, we go." Kyle said.

"We stay there, too. We might have to take you on that offer." Trey said.

"Alright, cool. Well, I'll let y'all get back to y'all workout and I'll see y'all around." Jackson said.

They gave us handshakes and walked out of the gym.

"Man, you're ready to hit the mall? To be honest, I'm too hyped you hit 550 like that. That messed up my mode from working out and shit. Let's hit the mall."

"Yeah, you're right. I'm about to go home and shower first." I said.

"Yeah, you had a good workout in. Damn bro, you're super strong, but how did you get that strong?" Trey asked.

"Well, I was raised on a farm. I had to push and pick up a bale of hay many times during the week and the bales weighed about 500 pounds, maybe more. I did that for years and it got easier overtime, plus digging up the soil and I did hit the weights as well. I also did a lot of pushups and ate pretty well." I said.

"Yeah, that makes sense. I bet your dad is big and strong too. Most of the time, it's DNA. Genes do play a big part of it." Trey said.

I started thinking and wondering what my real father looked like when Trey said that.

"Yeah, you're right, but let's get out of here before

another meathead challenges me again, haha." I said so I can skip the subject about talking about my father I never knew.

"Yeah, let's go. Plus I got a surprise for you too when we get home." Trey said.

"Alright, let's see what you got for me." I said.

"That's crazy. You're that strong. I mean, you do have a wide base and big hands. You play soccer, so I know you got some speed on you. What's your 40 time?" Trey asked as we were walking home.

"Well, if I told you, you wouldn't believe me." I said.

"Yeah, tell me," Trey said.

"I ran a 4.3 40 times." I said.

"Hold the fuck up, you benched 550? I didn't believe it until I saw it with my own eyes, and you have a 4.3, 40 times? I gotta see it. I mean, if you do man, you can go to the NFL. That 225 for 48 reps was crazy already."

"Yeah, but soccer is my dream, plus it's a lot safer. I've seen that movie, "Concussion" with Will Smith, haha. That's not going to be me. And soccer players make a lot of money as well, it's a lot safer." I said.

"Trust me, I understand. But, don't be surprised if football coaches will try to make you quit soccer for football." Trey said.

"They can try but, the answer is no, plus I know I'm going pro after this season, too. To go to the NFL, you gotta wait 3 seasons of college to go and the school will make money off you, doing those 3 seasons off ticket sales, jerseys and shirts with your name on it. That's millions of dollars they're making off you and you're not seeing a dime of it. The system is bogus, plus I could get hurt, they'll just throw it away and call me trash. I've seen it all the time. I have a family at home, I want to move out of the slums. The only sport I might do is Track because I love running and it can help my soccer resume." I said.

"Man, that's deep and you got a plan. I'm happy that you're sticking to it. You're right that's why I want my BBG company to hit. If I can get BBG nights at clubs all over the nation , even in different counties, that would be my dream, not the NFL. When that dream comes true, I get the feeling it's going to be soon. This morning in shirt sales, I woke up to 3,500 dollars of sales and it feels good to have a product people want. Like I said, when my dream comes true. I am out of this football shit for good." Trey said.

"Meek Mill said it the best. 'Self made, Self paid and I get myself a raise sound like your own boss.'" I said.

"You fuck with Meek? Stop playing, he's my favorite rapper. I fuck with Rick Ross music as well. I love his business moves as well. Him and Dame Dash are the biggest reasons, I'm going into business for myself. That interview I saw with Dame Do about being your own boss changed my life and one day, I will tell him that after I shake his hand." Trey said.

"It will happen one day." I said.

We made it home. I just wanted to jump in the shower and get dressed so I could see the mall and go shopping.

"Here, let me get that gift for you." Trey said.

I was wondering what he was getting for me. I checked my phone I get a text from Kendra, saying,

"Thank you for the good sex, I needed that. Sorry about my roommate, that's why I'm happy I'm moving into my own shit. Also, by the way, I talked to my friend that work at gym. She was wondering if you could come in for an interview at 9am tomorrow. Here is her number: 309-888-8880. Her name is Jasmine. She also said, 'give her a call when you can." Kendra texted.

"Yes, I needed that as well. Maybe I can be the first at your apartment and do you need help moving in? Also, thank you. I will call her for sure today." I texted.

"Hey dawg, you like this? I got a size XL made for you too."

"Thank you, I love it. I see you got Jamaican colors for me, too. It's your brand, BBG I see. I'm going to wear it right now."

"Thanks, dawg. That's love. But here, I'm about to shower, get dressed, then we can hit the mall. They have a nice food court, too. I'm hungry. Only thing I ate this morning was pussy, haha." Trey said with a laugh.

"I know. I heard you and your lady friend this morning, when I was getting ready to leave, haha." I said with a laugh.

"Dawg, I've been waiting to hit her ass since I moved on

campus. She got a fat ass too and she's dark skinned. I love chocolate women." Trey said.

"Ain't nothing wrong with chocolate in your life." I said.

"Yup, but I'm about to get ready." Trey said.

"Alright, me too." I said.

I walked in my room and got my clothes ready with the BBG shirt Trey gave me. I gave the gym girl Jasmine a call.

"Hello? Who is this?" Jasmine asked.

"My name is Eason. Kendra told me to give you a call about an interview tomorrow at 9am, about being a personal trainer?" I said.

"Yes, Kendra told me good things about you. Are you free at 9am for an interview?" Jasmine asked.

"Yes, I am. I'll be there for sure tomorrow." I said.

"Cool, I see you then. She told me you live at indigo apartments and the gym is actually close by, so that's good for you. Well, I'll see you tomorrow."

"Alright, see you tomorrow." I said.

I set my book bag on my bed and started taking everything out of it. They gave me 5fiveISU soccer team shirts and some ISU soccer shorts. I checked to see. It was a brown paper bag too, there was a note outside the brown paper bag. It was from Coach Woods. It read,

"Be safe this summer and protect yourself at all times."

I looked inside the brown paper bag and it was condoms;

a lot of them. Maybe over 50 of them. I just smiled and shook my head and said to myself, "I'm going to love college."

I got naked and got in the shower. I started thinking about Lisa, the white girl that wanted me to talk to her. I started picturing myself having sex with her. I got hard and started jacking off. I pictured myself fucking her doggy style. Pulling her hair while she screamed my name and moaned how great I felt...

I jacked off faster and faster. I came all over the shower floor while the water was splashing on my abs and dick. I washed the rest of my body off and stopped the shower to dry off as I went to get dressed. I put lotion on with cocoa butter and got dressed. I put on my Jamaican snap back with the Jamaica color BBG shirt Trey gave me. Then I also took 1,000 dollars out of the 5,500 that was given to me and I put that money in a drawer, in a sock. I forgot I just had it and my shorts pocket. The last thing I want to do is lose this much money, so I put it up.

I texted Lisa to see what she was doing. I also texted her, "Hey, how are you doing?' This is Eason the Jamaican guy."

I then went into the living room to see if Trey was ready. Trey came out ready, wearing his BBG shirt, red and white Nike's.

"Let's go. That shirt fits nicely. Wish my arms were big like yours. I need to hit the curls more, I guess." Trey said.

"My arms are alright, but I want tattoos like you." I said.

"Well, I know a few tattoo artists at this shop. We can stop by there after the mall. I talked to them about getting my chest done." Trey said.

"Cool, I am down for that." I said.

"Well, let's go. We might see some girls we might like at the mall too."

So we left our apartment and got in. The color of Trey's Jeep was the color red like our school colors. We drove to the mall and he started playing Meek Mill's, "Dreams and Nightmares" song. We both started singing the song like we made the song ourselves. The song kept playing.

Beep, I checked my phone and I got a text from Lisa saying, "Hey handsome with the green eyes, What are you up to?" She asked with a smiling face.

I texted back and said, "on my way to the mall to go shopping and also checking on getting some tattoos." I texted.

Driving past, I looked around, saw restaurants and car lots. Places I've never seen before. It was a new world for me. People driving cars, the sun was hot and it was a nice sunny day like it was in Jamaica.

"There's the mall, we made it." Trey said.

I looked and the place was big outside. I've never seen a place like it. There were a lot of cars in the parking lot. Our malls in Jamaica don't look like this at all.

Beep, I got a text from Kendra. "Sorry about the late text, but no thank you. My dad and uncle are helping me move in.

You're such a gentleman though." Kendra said.

Enjoying Summer

CHAPTER 3

We walked in the mall and the inside was big. I saw three floors. When I looked up, people were shopping. There were all kinds of clothing stores and shoe stores. I had a big smile on my face. I had 1,000 dollars in my pockets. I'm about to buy clothes and shoes so I can start out my freshman year of college.

"Let's hit the food court up, I want some Chinese." Trey said.

"Alright, I'll get what you get. I'm not a picky eater at all." I said.

We walked our way to the food court, then I saw a thick brown skin woman with long dreadlocks walking past me. Her curves were on point. She was on the BBW side, but I didn't mind a woman with some meat on her bones. I looked her up and down and she looked at me too with a smile. I could tell she was older than me, maybe in her mid 30s, but I didn't care at all. I looked at her ass and it moved like it was a water balloon. Her nails were done and she had pretty feet, too. As I was looking at this woman up and down, I told myself, "if it was meant for me to meet her, I would see her again."

"It looks like the China man line is packed but it's worth the wait."

We got in line and saw two pretty black women, pointing at us and coming our way while we were in line.

"Excuse me, we love y'all shirts! Where can we get them?" One of them asked.

"You can order them off my website. It's my clothing brand, 'BBG (Big Booty Gang).' Here, take my business card. All of the info you need is there."

"Big booty gang. Well, I think our asses are big enough to wear the brand. What do you think?" One of the girls asked

They turn their asses around so we can look at them.

"Yes, your ass is perfect and nice I see." Trey said with a smile.

"Y'all are some cuties. Where y'all from? Y'all must be football players at the University? My name is Nisha, by the way." Nisha said.

"Well, my name is Trey and I'm from Chicago. Yes, I do play football at ISU."

"My name is Eason. I am from Jamaica and I play soccer. What about y'all?"

"I love your accent and your green eyes. I never meant a dark skin brother with green eyes. But nope, we don't go to college. I own a hair salon. I love your dreads. I can braid them up for you and give you a nice lining too." Nisha said with a smile.

"Yes, she can hook you up and I can cut your hair, light skin. My name is Kelly and I work at her salon. I do hair and cut it, also. I love your waves by the way." Kelly said with a smile on her face.

Me and Trey looked at each other, thinking the same thing. I'm pretty sure it was about having sex with these big booty women.

"Yes, we would love to check your salon out. And, yes Kelly, I've been looking for a person to cut my hair since I moved here. What's your number?" He asked Kelly.

"Well, I've never tried to braid my dreads before, but I want to do it. Maybe tomorrow, I'll come by." I said to Nisha.

"Sure, come by. Here is my business card and I'll be waiting to hear from you. Looks like y'all are next in line. So I'll talk to you later, handsome. Have a good one." Nisha said.

They walked off and Trey watched, looking at their booties like creeps.

"Boy, these sisters were bad. Yeah, we're going to hit, but let's order. Dude looking at us, pissed off with his, 'hurry up and order' head ass." Trey said.

"May I take your order?" The cashier asked.

"Yes, I would like: the orange chicken, fried rice, egg foo young with a large lemonade to go, please." Trey said.

"Why did you ask for it to go if we're eating here?" I asked.

"I'll tell you when we sit down, but order it to go. Trust me, I got you." Trey said.

"I'm going to have the same thing he's having with a large lemonade too." I said.

Trey paid for our food, then went to sit down to eat.

"Thank you for paying for my food again, I could have paid for it." I said.

"It's cool. You can pay for the next few meals, it's no trouble. I'm in a grateful place in my life now. From the hell I've been through, I'm making good money. My shirts are selling out. Just two years ago before my last college. I was actually homeless, sleeping place to place. Sleeping at parks, wearing the same dirty clothes with dirty and old sweat on them that smelled bad. Missing meals because of my dream. I lost my apartment and my car. I had a Jeep and got a repo. I just kept failing because I wanted to quit my dream. Sleeping on people's floors, crying myself to sleep, feeling less than a man." Trey said.

"Wow, I would have never known. You don't even look like you've been through such pain, how did you get out of it?" I asked.

"Well my family didn't know, but they didn't have money anyways to help, so I didn't tell them. I ended up sleeping on an old friend's floor, working as a cashier in McDonald's. At the same time, I didn't care. I just wanted to get myself together, but the old friend I was living with, his family was using me. By finding out, I was over paying for bills because the landlord told me I should start thinking about getting out of here, but how? I started thinking. When I was at work, one of my coworkers was talking about this two-year college he visited that had dorms and it's easy to get in. He said he didn't like the college, plus it was in the middle of nowhere in Illinois. The football program sucked, too. So he didn't want to go. I asked him the town and the college's name. He said, "It was Jacksonville, IL and the college name was Jacksonville College.

It's about a hour and a half away from here, but I take back roads so I can get here in 45 mins. Right then and there, I went on google, got the number and called the school. They said they were a two year college with housing, so I applied at the college. Send them whatever they need. Talked to the football coach. He said I wanted to walk-on. He said he needed linebackers and he learned my height and weight.

I asked to move in early once I got accepted because I told him I wanted to move in a better environment and wanted to get better workouts to focus on football. He said he didn't have any problem with that, plus I was already lifting weights again, getting my body back together anyway. Once I got accepted, it was summer time anyway, school was in two months, so I paid for my greyhound ticket, packed my clothes in a garbage bag and I was gone. I took Advantage of the opportunity that was given to me. I did well in football at the college and I got good grades. I started promoting my brand again the right way and I was able to buy myself a Jeep and my grades helped me to get here." Trey said.

"Wow, your story is amazing. I hope you get where you're trying to go. I hope you get interviewed one day so you can tell your story." I said.

"Yeah, maybe I will one day be on a major radio station." Trey said.

"What about you? What's your story, dawg." Trey asked.

I told Trey everything about my life. I trusted him. I could tell he was a good person. Him telling me what he'd been through made me comfortable to tell him about my life.

"Damn dawg and I thought I had it bad. You had it really bad and you did not know your real parents either? That's ruff, but God tests the strongest soldiers. One day, you'll see we all have a journey. Everyone's journey is different. I got family members that don't want me doing what I'm doing. They want me to work a normal 9 to 5 for the rest of my life. I tried 9 to 5 life. It isn't for me. God just made us different. We ain't better than anyone else, but he just made us different." Trey said.

"Yeah, that's why I'm thankful where I'm at right now and I know things will get better." I said.

" That's right, now let's finish our food so we can hit these stores up." Trey said.

After we finished eating, I bought clothes I've never had before. I got me some nice polos and V-necks. I got name brand underwear, tank tops and socks. I got new shoes, white Air Force ones and some Jordan's. A guy called me over to smell cologne and I got that too. I also got a gold watch and a gold cross chain. I also got earrings. I had bags of new stuff. Trey did too.

"Hey, I just got a text about a party at this club downtown, I think we should go." Trey said.

"Yes, I want to go." I said.

"Cool. Well, I'm done getting what I want. Let's get ready for it." Trey said.

We left the mall. We went back home and I got a text from Lisa.

"What are you doing later?" Lisa texted.

"Going to a club later, what about you?" I texted.

"You should come over before you go to the club. I want to talk to you in person, handsome." Lisa texted with a smile on her face.

"Hey Trey, that girl Lisa wants me to come over before we hit the club." I said.

"Damn, yeah you better bring a condom with you because she wants you to smash real quick." Trey said.

"Yeah, she does have a nice body and she is sexy. That white dude Jordan, is going to be pissed off if he finds out." I said.

"Damn, he is going to be pissed dawg, but oh well hahaha. Fuck dude and speaking of dude, he's pissed anyway at you more because they posted of a video of you lifting 225lbs 48 times and showed you bench pressing 550. Social media is going crazy in the comments. People saying they saw you on campus already man. You're about to be famous on campus." Trey said.

"Well, I wasn't trying to show off at all." I said.

"Naw, you wasn't but people will respect you and hate you at the same time. But anyways, take your time with that Lisa girl. We're not leaving till 10:30 pm anyway and it's only 6:00 p.m." Trey said.

"Alright Cool, I can't wait to see the club." I said.

We made it home and I went to put my stuff up in my room. I text Lisa, asking her where she lived.

She texted back and said, "A house, but I can pick you up if you need me too." I told her, "Yes, please. Pick me up and I'll gave her my address."

She texted me and told me she'll be here in 10 mins. Trey and I got our bags, and went inside our place.

"The name of this club is called, "Rush." Pretty much a lot of people from the game are going to be there. I hope they don't play any lame ass music, because the bars at Jacksonville were lame as hell. Nothing really to do at all, that's another reason I left. Also, reading more about it, they're page said it's a reggae party. Awww shit, they're going to be playing your type of music." Trey said.

"Reggae party huh? I have to see this." I said.

Beep, got a text from Lisa "I'm here." Lisa's text read.

"Welp, I'll be seeing you later. Let me put these bags here right quick, Lisa is here." I said.

"Well, do your thing. I'll see you tonight" Trey said.

I put my bags up and got a few condoms. I went downstairs and saw her in a black BMW. I started thinking to myself she got money. I went inside the car, she was wearing ISU softball sweatpants and a ISU softball t-shirt. She smelled good, too.

"Sorry that I am down dressed but, I just got out of the shower from working out. I just wanted some company, maybe to get to know each other, just have some convo's and Netflix and chill." Lisa said.

"Sure, I am down for that." I said.

We left my place and she drove to her place.

"So, I've been seeing your video all over social media. You had Jordan pissed. He likes me, but he isn't my type. I have to give it to you. You are strong. I'm surprised you don't play football. You got the size for it, that's for sure." Lisa said.

"Yeah, I've been told, but soccer is my sport. In Jamaica, the sport of soccer is big. Same as track and field. In Jamaica, we have soccer and track. In America, they have basketball and football." I said.

"Yeah, that makes sense. Soccer is very big across the world and they get paid pretty well too. I went to high school with a kid from Mexico. He came from a very poor background after high school. He did a year of college at some small school and got drafted to the MLS. Now, he and his family are living a better life because of him." Lisa said.

"Good for him, that's the same plan I have. To go pro after one season." I said.

"Pro, huh? After one season? You must be good. I will make sure to check your games out. Well, we made it to my house." Lisa said.

I looked and it was a nice sized house on the outside. We got out of the car and went inside her house. It was nice inside, also. She had brown furniture and wooden floors.

"You have a nice house. This house is yours, by yourself?" I asked.

"Yes, my dad got it for me my freshman year of college. I didn't want to live in a dorm at all so he brought it for me. It's my last year. I'm graduating. He's going to sell the house when I move out." Lisa said.

"Well, you must have some rich parents." I said.

"Well, I guess. My dad is in the oil business and owns an oil company. My mom is a real estate broker." Lisa said.

"Wow, that's good for them. What are your plans after college?" I asked.

"Well, I'm getting a degree in business marketing to promote and help brand his oil business, so I'm going to work for him right after college."

"Wow, that's amazing." I said with a smile.

I started thinking to myself like I wish I had it good like her. It sounded like she had a nice childhood, but I knew my journey was different and my life was different.

"Here, let's go to my room." Lisa said.

I followed her into her room. It was big with a king size bed. She had softball posters up of herself. I also saw trophies as well. She also had a big screen TV. Her room was pretty much red and white like the school colors.

"I see you must be good at softball with all these trophies, plus I see you love seeing yourself on the wall, haha." I said with a laugh.

"I see you got jokes but yes, I've been playing softball since I was in elementary. It helped me get a full ride to ISU. It was a tool for a free education, you know."

"Yeah, I can understand that, that's for sure." I said.

"Here, let's lay on my bed and watch TV." Lisa said.

I looked at how thick she was in her sweat pants and I started getting hard. It looked so soft and round.

"Sure." I said.

She got under the cover.

"You can get under the covers with me, too."

She didn't have to tell me twice. So, I got under the covers and cuddled with her.

"Let's see what movie there is to watch. I'm getting hot, I hope you don't mind me taking my sweatpants off."

"Sure, it's your house." I said.

She took her sweatpants off and she was wearing a black thong. Once I saw that, it got hard. Like my dick wanted to grab her closer to me. She went to turn her bedroom light off and got back to bed with me. She put her ass on my hard dick.

"You smell nice and feel good, I hope you don't mind. I like being close to your skin, it just feels nice." she said.

My dick was rubbing against her ass and it started throbbing. We both started watching TV, but I wasn't focused on the TV.

"Mmm, looks like someone down there is saying hello," she said.

Then, she came closer to me to put her ass on me more and start grinding on me. Then, I started grinding back. She put her hand under the cover and started touching my dick slowly and softly. Her hands felt good. She touched my balls and went back to touching my dick with just two fingers. She went down to the base, then she came back up to the tip.

"Wow. if I counted right, you have 9 inches of dick laying against my ass," she said.

"Last time I checked, yes I do."

"Nice, real nice. May I kiss it please?" She asked.

"You want to kiss my dick?", I asked.

"Yes and your balls too please." she said.

"Sure." I said.

I laid on my back, she went under the covers and started kissing my dick. Then she made her way to my balls with her tongue and kissed each ball. I started moaning a little bit. She used her hands and jacked my dick off while licking my balls real fast.

"You have very big balls I see, that's sexy," she said.

Then she started sucking my dick slowly and I put my hand on her head while she went up and down on my dick. After that, she started moaning while sucking my dick. I put my other hand on her head and started stroking her mouth faster like I was having sex with her mouth. She moaned louder and she stopped.

"Did you have a condom?" She asked.

"Yes I do, but before I fuck, may I kiss your pussy for a little bit?" I asked.

"Yes please, I thought you would've never offered." She said.

"No, it would be my pleasure." I said.

I started making my way to her pussy and I started kissing her pussy lips. She started moaning and cussing.

"Yes, please baby keep going, OMG!!! Keep going."

I started french kissing her pussy lips. I put my tongue around her lips, started licking her clique fast, she put her hands in my dreads and started grabbing them tight.

"Yes, I'm about to cum go faster please go faster." she said.

I looked up and her eyes were closed. I put my hands on her tities while eating her pussy at the same time.

"Yes, Eason I'm cumming, I'm cumming!" She yelled.

Then she came hard all over my mouth. She grabbed the sheets tight while catching her breath.

"Put a condom on and do what you want to me."

I got off the bed, walked to my shorts pocket and put a condom on. I walked up to her and put her legs on my shoulders. Picked her up for a ride she was going to enjoy. I started fucking her while standing up. All you heard was her ass clapping and her moaning.

"Yes, omg. You feel so good. Give me that black cock, please keep going!!" She yelled.

I started going faster and faster. She held my shoulders tighter so she could enjoy the ride.

"Please Eason, keep going yesssss! Keep going, I'm about to cum again, omg!"

I went faster while her ass cheeks were slapping against my balls and I knew I was coming close to cumming.

"Yes, I'm cumming again, Eason yes, please don't stop."

I kept going and her blue eyes locked on my green eyes as she moaned and screamed she's about to cum.

"Let me know when you cum so I can cum, too." I said.

"I'm cumming now, right now, I'm cumming right now!" She screamed.

I went faster and I started moaning.

I'm cumming too. Then, we both came at the same time while looking at each other.

"Wow, that was great. I needed that. You're actually the best I've ever had and the biggest I've ever had. You Jamaican men can put it down I see." She said with a smile.

" Why Thank you, you're pretty good yourself." I said.

"Yeah, here. Do you want a Powerade or something to drink?" She said.

"Sure, that would be nice." I said.

I looked at the time it was 8:30 pm.

"Here you go and we have to go. My dad is on his way. I didn't know he was coming. I hate to say this but, he's racist and would kill me if he found you're here." Lisa said with a worried look.

"Alright, let's go. I have to get ready for the club anyway." I said.

We got dressed and got in her car. She pulled off her driveway to take me home.

"Sorry about me rushing you home." Lisa said.

"So he hates black people, I take it?" I asked.

"Yes, he does but I'm not racist at all." Lisa said.

"Well, what's going to happen if you want a black husband one day?" I asked.

"I ask myself that all the time and if I do marry a black man, he would cut me off from the family and he wouldn't hire me at all for his business. He would have started me off with a 95,000 a year salary." Lisa said.

I started thinking to myself like wow. 95,000 a year salary? That's a lot of money, but he's basically controlling her life and who she should date or talk to. Just sad how people can be so hateful.

"Only thing I can say is, is your happiness worth 95,000 a year? Your soulmate might be a black man, you just never know. That's all I'm going to say.

Well, I had a great time with you and I'll talk to you later. Thanks for the ride." I said.

"Thanks and I will talk to you later." Lisa said.

I went upstairs and went inside my apartment. I saw Trey eating pizza and watching tv.

"Hey dawg, you had a good time? And I know you're hungry here. The pizza just came. I'm not going to eat all of this, haha." Trey said with a smile.

"Yeah, we had a cool time, but she started telling me her father was on her way. I had to leave because he's racist and doesn't like black people at all." I said.

"Yeah man, you have to get used to that here in America. It's a lot more white kids at this university than black kids. Some of them come from small ass farm towns that black people don't live in. So when they come to college and see us, it's different to them. Some of them will want to get to know you because they play our music and watch us on TV. Some of them just love black culture and want to understand us and give us respect. Then, you got some that were brainwashed with hate, so they judge us before they know us without giving us a chance. I'm just used to it. I've been called 'Nigger' so many times, growing up. It doesn't even hurt me anymore because I know for a fact if they knew me, they wouldn't say such things, you know." Trey said.

Trey was saying some deep stuff. I could tell he was used to living in a society like this and it didn't get to him.

"So, it doesn't get to you?" I asked.

"It used to, but at the end of the day, I'm a man and I'm not going to have another man have power over me by calling me names or feeling a way about me. If they don't put their hands on me, then we are cool. Talk away, say what you want. But at the end of the day, I'm the better man because I'm going to go home and live my life, dawg. God had blessed me. He made a strong, handsome black man with intelligence to do what I want with my life and I'm going to do it; I'm going to live." Trey said with passion.

"I can understand that. I haven't been call a 'Nigger' before, but I hope I can be understanding like you." I said.

"Trust me, it's going to come. I don't know when, but racist shit will happen to you. It's a part of living in America. It's sad, but this country was made off of racism, so get used to it, but other than that, America can be an amazing place. You have the freedom to do and say what you want. Like I said before, it's white people that respect you and will judge you based on your character in actions, not how you look." Trey said.

"That's good to hear. But, let me get dressed and brush my teeth. My breath smells like pussy, I bet." I said.

"I heard that play boy, I'm about to get ready as well and Kelly text me. The girl that cut hair. I told her I'll come by tomorrow to get a haircut." Trey said.

"Yeah, I might come as well." I said.

I finished eating the pizza and went into my room to get dressed. I got my outfit ready for tonight. It was a Jamaican color Ralph.

Lauren polo with Ralph Lauren, white shorts, also white polo socks and white Air Force ones. All I got today from the mall. I've checked that I had 400 dollars left in my wallet and I set my wallet with my clothes. I also got new polo underwear as well. I was about to be fresh tonight. I went on the floor and did 100 push ups, got naked and took a shower. After my shower, I washed my mouth out and brushed my teeth. I didn't want my breath smelling like pussy while talking to women. I got dressed and put cologne on as well. The polo fit nicely around my arms and the gold watch as well. It was an Ivan Davon watch. It came with my earrings. I was looking good. I went into the living room and I saw Trey was dressed as well. It was nice to go.

"I see you wearing that Jamaican polo. That's nice, dawg. Let's take some shots of Ciroc. I got some coconut flavor, too. I like to be buzzed before I go to the club." Trey said.

Trey went in the freezer and took a big bottle of Ciroc out. We both took 5 shots, left and went to his Jeep. We were gone. Then, I got a text from Kendra.

"Hey how are you doing, handsome? I'm all moved into my new place." Kendra texted.

"I'm with Trey, headed to the club. eIt's reggae night. I'm going to have to check out your new place." I texted with a smile on my face.

"Sure, if you want to after the club, come by. I'll show you around. I know you have an interview tomorrow, so you can spend the night if you want to." Kendra texted.

"Sure, give me the address sexy." I said.

"478 N Woodview. It's not that far from indigo apartments either, call me when you're on your way." She texted.

"What's this song you got playing? I like it!" I said.

"A new artist called Pop Smoke. The song is called 'Welcome to the Party'. Nicki Minaj just remixed it, too. This shit is fire dawg." Trey said.

"I'm feeling it, turn it up." I said.

I saw a group of women walking to a club and I saw people waiting in line as well.

"We made it here. Damn, it's getting packed. I'm looking for a parking spot now so we can get in line before the line gets longer." Trey said.

"So we found a parking spot and parked next to some girls. There were four of them coming out of this white jeep, the same jeep as Trey's.

"Here is some winter fresh gum just in case, I know one of them girls that got out of the jeep next to us!" Trey said.

"How do you know her?" I asked.

"She went to Jacksonville college with me. I see she's hanging with the Alpha Alpha Alpha girls." Trey said.

"What's that?" I asked.

"Alpha Alpha Alpha" is a sorority where you have to be very pretty to join. They say you don't have to be pretty. But to be honest, I've never seen an ugly Alpha girl, plus I heard this one chick was trying to join and she happened to be ugly. They told her she was too ugly to join and joined another sorority. Shit was crazy. Like my uncle likes to say, they are the pretty hoes on campus.

"I see! This is all new to me, but I'm pretty sure I got all my college years to learn about this stuff." I said.

We got out of the Jeep and started walking to the club to get in line. Then, we made it in line and we were next to the Alpha Girls. One looked at us and said something to her friends.

"Hey Trey, I heard you got into ISU! And, you're playing football here." She said,

"Yeah. Are you going to school here too?" Trey asked.

"Yes, I am. Who is your friend, he's your teammate?" She asked.

"You can talk to me, I don't bite and I actually play soccer. My name is Eason. What is your name?" I asked.

"My name is Star and wow, a soccer player. You look like you play football." Star said.

"Yeah, I get that a lot. But, I moved here from Jamaica to play soccer." I said.

"Wow Jamaican, huh? I can hear the accent and I love your dreadlocks, my Jamaican King. I am in love with your green eyes, too. You're a very handsome brother." Star said with a smile.

"Girl, stop flirting with this tall, dark and handsome man. We're up next, haha." Alpha girl said with a laugh and smile.

"Girl, you see how tall and fine that motherfucker is though? Plus, He's from Jamaica. I need that in my life. Shit the light skinned friend is sexy, too. I like them big ass arms and tattoos he has." Alpha girls said.

"They seem nice." I said.

"Yeah, they look good. Star is cool people. She might be single now. She was dating a teammate of mine. I'm pretty sure they broke up, though. She's all for you." Trey said.

"That's cool, man. It's packed out here and the music is loud. Can't wait to see the inside." I said.

"ID's please." The *bouncer* said.

I took out my passport and Trey took out his ID. The Bouncer looked at them and let us in. When we got in, it was packed and they were playing reggae music I've heard before. I saw people dancing and having a good time.

"Hey, dance with me." Star asked.

"Alright." I said.

"Hundred Hundred on this Hundred Hundred on that". I started hearing Safaree's 'Hundred song'. A song I really loved and I started dancing. Doing a dance called the Reggae Stroll. Once I started, I started hearing people saying, "Aye, Aye, Ayeeee, ayeee!" People came behind and started doing the dance with me.

"You're a good dancer, I see. I mean, you are from a party island." Star said.

Star was about 5'7 tall, slim thick with a smooth dark skin tone, with long braids. Very pretty. She favored the singer, Kelly

Rowland.

"Yeah, we do a lot of dancing where we are from, so have you been to Jamaica before?" I asked.

"No, I haven't, but I will go one day. Here, give me your phone. We are going to be new friends." She said.

I gave her my phone and she put her number in. Then she gave me my phone back and we finished dancing, as she put her ass on my dick and started shaking it. She looked back at her ass and started smiling. I know she can feel my dick rubbing against her ass and I started humping it like I was in a bedroom, making love to her doggy style, but with dry humping.

"You better stop before you start something you can't finish, big boy." Star turned around and said.

"I always finish what I start." I said with a smile.

"Alright, hit me up and prove it sometime, then. Looks like my friends are leaving. Hit me up sometime, Jamaican King." Star said.

"I will do that." I said.

I went to see where Trey was at. I saw him talking to two latin women by the bar, drinking a beer. I walked over.

"Hey, I was just talking about you, they are both from Puerto Rico. I was telling them that you're from Jamaica." Trey said.

"Hey, papi. My name is Isabel and this is my cousin, Kila." Isabel said.

"Nice to meet y'all." I said.

Isabel started touching my arms. She was about 5'4 short, but very thick on the bbw side, with a nice smile; very pretty. Also had long, dark curly hair.

"You're very beautiful and your eyes make me very weak. You're tall and big. Just how I like it." Isabel said.

"Why, thank you. I love your smile and your lovely curves." I said.

"Why, thank you, sexy. So how have you been liking reggae night so far?" Isabel asked.

"I'm loving it, the vibe and music. Whoever put this together, they knew what they were doing. I need to thank the owner for having such a night." I said.

"Well, maybe you can thank me now." Isabel said.

"You're the owner of the club?" I asked, looking surprised.

"Yes, I am. I've been here about 5 years now. Let me show you around. Trey and my cousin will be alright. It Looks like they like each other." Isabel said.

So she showed me around the club. It was a nice layout, but I was looking at her curves, up and down hard. She was touching on me and I was touching on her.

"Here, let me show you upstairs." Isabel said.

We walked past the dance floor and she unlocked this door. As we were walking up the stairs, her big booty was all in my face. I wanted to bite it. She opened another door and then the light came on. It was an apartment I had never seen before. An apartment upstairs from a club.

"This is my apartment, do you like it?" Isabel asked.

"Wow, it's nice. I love the white furniture theme you got going on here. I've never seen an apartment connected to a club before. Must be nice to live where you work." I said.

"Yes, it is. I own the building. Believe it or not, I used to work at a place called King Burger." Isabel said.

"Yes, I love their burgers. You used to work there?" I asked.

"Yes. I come from a poor background. College wasn't for me, but I always wanted to own a club. I was saving my money for awhile, but not even close to buying a club. I learned that good credit can buy you anything. I knew I couldn't save up for the club, but I can get good credit. It took me a few years, but I got my credit score close to 800 and got a business loan of 350,000, once I knew I was approved. Then I saw that this building was for sale for 200,000. The club before wasn't doing that well in sales. The last club owner said he told me how much he would sell the building for and I got the money for him. He was going through hard times. Anyway, I came just in time and talked down to 150,000. It took me a while to get stuff in order for the club, but once I did, things started coming up right. I hated working at that damn burger joint. Being told what to do, begging for a day off... It's not in my blood to be a worker and my living situation wasn't the best. I was sleeping on the floor with other cousins and had to share the bathroom with 6 other people. It was annoying, but I don't have to do that anymore, thank God." Isabel said.

"Wow, that's amazing. Trust me, I know about sleeping on the floor and sharing a bathroom with other people. It can be annoying, so you own the building, That means no rent. You just have to pay property taxes and you can work at a dead end job and pay that. That's great. I'm happy for your success." I said.

"Why, thank you and yes, no rent and I see that you're into real estate. What's your major?" Isabel asked.

"Business Management, but I'm not getting a degree. I don't need it for the plans I have in my life, plus I'm a soccer player." I said.

"You came all the way here from Jamaica to play soccer and not get a degree?" Isabel asked.

"Yup." I said.

"You must be good; you must be planning on going pro?" Isabel asked.

"Yes, that's the plan after this season." I said.

"I have to come to one of your games and check you out, then. I'm a soccer fan as well. I'm all for team Puerto Rico over here." Isabel said with a smile.

"Yeah, they have a good team, but not like the Rasta Boyz. One day I'm going to help take them to a World Cup some day."

"That's a good dream. Maybe one day, I'll come to that World Cup game and you can take off that winning jersey to autograph it for me, so I can sell it for a million dollars, haha." Isabel said while laughing.

"You better not sell it, you're supposed to frame it, haha." I said with a laugh.

I was feeling Isabel. We kept talking. We sat on her white couch and got closer. She felt on me and I felt on her. Then, I grab her soft big booty. I got hard right then and there.

"I see you like my booty a lot." Isabel said.

"Yes I do." I said.

"Here, come here. I was to tell you something in your ear." Isabel said.

She licked my ear and whispered in it.

"You're wearing white shorts and I can see your big dick through your shorts. Maybe it needs some air. You should take it out for me." Isabel said in a sexy voice.

So I stood up,unbuckled my belt and shorts and pulled my shorts down. She was sitting down and she moved closer to pull my underwear down. She saw how my dick was twitching at her. She got some baby oil that was next to her on the floor and poured some in her hand. She rubbed them together, starting to massage my dick and balls. She wasn't ruff at all. She pulled her face closer to my dick and kept massaging it.

"You have a nice big dick and big balls. Everything I hear about Jamaican men is true. I see why some men envy y'all. Here, come closer." Isabel said.

She started sucking my dick slowly. I started moaning.

"You like that, papi?" Isabel asked.

"Yes, I do a lot." I said.

"I want you to fuck me doggy style and pull my hair while slapping my ass, papi." Isabel said.

She got up and turned around. Pulled her pants down, pulled her blue thongs down to her knees and got on the couch. I put a condom on and slapped my dick on her booty cheeks and put my dick inside her pussy as she started to moan.

"Yes, papi keep going please." Isabel moaned.

My balls were slapping against her pussy while I was pulling her hair. Her tan body and her dark hair was a turn on. She looked back at her ass and at me when I was giving her backshots, then she started talking in Spanish.

"Vaya más rápido, vaya más rápido, vaya más rápido! It means go faster, go faster, go faster!" Isabel was moaning.

Her pussy felt so warm like I was dipping my dick in warm, Caribbean water that was in 100 degree weather. She told me to stop while she would sit on my dick like a chair. She went up and down, up and down. All I saw was ass on my lap. She would also go side to side on my dick.

Papi, por favor cum meaning please cum now. She kept

going up and down. I grabbed her double D titties, licked behind her ear and neck while holding her close. She moaned and I moaned as we both came together.

"Damn, that was good, papi. Go clean yourself up in the bathroom, just in case you have a girlfriend or something. I don't want you in trouble. Towels are in the bathroom." Isabel said.

"Well, I'm single but I will go clean. Damn you're good. I love how you flop your ass on me. I'm going to have to see you again." I said.

"You can, that's for sure. I got a text from my cousin. She is looking for me. Let's hurry up, sexy. Here, take my number and hit me up sometimes." Isabel said.

So I went to the bathroom to wash my balls and dick, then I used her mouthwash as well. She went to clean up when I was done. We went back to the club. It got more packed and I saw Trey getting into it with three guys. So I ran over there to see what was going on.

"Hey Trey, what's going on?" I asked with a serious voice.

"These niggas on some hating ass shit because girls are talking to me. Tthese weird ass niggas been trying to talk to hoes all night and ain't getting no play!" Trey said in an angry tone.

"If the ladies don't want y'all, don't hate the playa, hate the game, fellas. Y'all should leave before it gets real serious in this club. Security is coming over here." I said in a serious voice.

"Whatever, y'all ain't on shit anyway. Let's go, y'all. We'll see them around." One of them said and they left.

"Damn, I got back just in time, I see." I said.

"Yeah, you did dawg. Three versus one is kind of hard, but when you came, I guess they changed their mind. But, fuck them niggas. The Alpha Girls and Star want to go to the Pancake House, and want us to come with them." Trey said.

"Sure, I can eat. Where are they?" I asked.

"They're meeting us there. They are on their way there now. Star was looking for you, but I said you went to the bathroom. I knew you were with Isabel and she was showing you around." Trey said.

"Yeah she was and we danced a bit as well." I said, knowing I don't kiss or tell.

"Cool. Let's get out of here. It's about 1:30 am. The club closes at 2 am. It's packed as hell in here and I know it's going to be hell, trying to get out when they close. Get the jeep out of here, too. Let's hit it bro, plus I want one of them Alpha girls." Trey said.

So we left the club and got in the Jeep to leave.

Summer Passion

CHAPTER 4

When we got to the pancake house, it was packed as well. I looked on the side and the Alpha girls were waving at us to come over as we walked over.

"Hey, y'all! Come over here. We got room for y'all. Y'all just came just in time." Star said.

"Yeah, we see. I'm going to sit next to you, beautiful face." Trey said to one of the Alpha girls.

"Hey my Jamaican King, sit next to me." Star said.

"Hey y'all, I'm Eason by the way. I didn't get a chance to talk to any of y'all when we were at the club." I said to the Alpha girls.

"I'm Tara and I've been to Jamaica before. It was paradise. Which part of Jamaica are you from and why do you have green eyes?" Tara asked.

"Well, I'm from Kingston, but grew up on the country side of things and my green eyes? I don't know, to be honest." I said.

"I'm Judy. So you're the soccer player I heard, but I saw a video of you lifting heavy ass weights like a football player." Judy said.

"Yeah, I saw that video, too. It was over 500 pounds. I didn't know that was you. Damn, you're a strong kid. What were they feeding you, growing up? And sorry, my name is Nicki." Nicki said.

"Well, I grew up on a farm. So I ate pretty good." I said.

"Your accent is nice and you have nice white teeth, too. Boy, when school starts, the hoes are going to be all over your ass. Don't be surprised if one of the frats asks you to join." Nicki said.

"Well, I'm going to be too busy playing soccer and doing school work. Plus after the year, I'm going pro. So I won't be here long." I said.

"Pro!!! Damn, you must be good. You're going to pull one and done on us? I heard that basketball players do it all the time. I didn't know you could do that in soccer as well. Soccer is big in Jamaica, so it only makes sense why you'd play the sport." Star said.

"Yup, you can go pro right after high school if you wanted to! I wanted to come to America to see how it was here."

"Hello, my name is Gee and I will be taking your order. May I get your drinks? Are you guys ready now?"

We started giving our orders and I saw Star looking at her wallet. I saw like 5 dollars in there and I saw her looking at things less than 5 dollars so I whispered at her,

"Get what you want, I'm paying for your food." I said.

"You sure?" Star asked.

"Yes I'm sure, I have enough money to pay for you. Where I'm from, we want everybody to be full, so get anything you want, I got you." I said to her.

"Thank you." Star said.

I ordered my food and Star did, too. She ordered a steak, egg and pancakes meal. I could tell she must have been hungry. The waiter took our orders and left.

"Hey, Trey. I see you all over Judy. You better be nice to her." Star said.

"I'm always nice." Trey said with a smile.

"Yeah, you're right. Your old teammate wasn't nice. The nigga cheated on me with 5 different girls at the school and got two of them pregnant. He had to drop out and get a job at some factory last time I heard." Star said.

"Damn!!!! I didn't know he was doing you dirty like that and that's crazy. Around the end of spring semester, I didn't see him at all." Trey said.

"Yeah, that's when he found out everything and even took a D.N.A test to make sure and they both were his, so he dropped out. I felt sorry for him, even though I was mad as hell, but he was a smart dude and wanted to be an engineer. When you have two baby mommas and their family comes at you, you gotta take care of business. Now he's working a job he hates. Last time we spoke, he said he was sorry and wanted to work things out. I told him 'no thank you' and kept it moving." Star said.

"Damn, that's crazy. Coach always told us to wear condoms, it will save your life and save you a lot of money in the long run." Trey said.

"Hey, y'all should come to the Chicago beach party with us this weekend. There's going to be a BBQ there, drinks, music and a volleyball tournament this Saturday." Nicki said.

"Yeah, I'm down for that. What about you, Eason?" Trey asked.

"Sure, it sounds like it will be a great time. I've always wanted to go to Chicago anyway." I said.

"Cool, I'll send y'all the details. Look, the food is here, about time. I'm hungry as hell." Nicki said.

We all got our food and enjoyed each other's company. They told me about how long they will be in the sorority and their plans after college. They were some cool black women with ambition and dreams to make it to the top, even Star and I talked for a bit as well. I didn't want a one night stand with her at all. I got a text from Kendra. It was about 2:30 am. She asked if I wanted to come over this late as I started thinking to myself that I've already slept with 2 women today. But, then she texted me a picture of her wearing just a rode naked. I told her I'll be right over. The pancake house was getting ready to close anyway. We got done eating. Paid for our food and left the parking lot for our cars.

"It was nice meeting y'all. I see y'all Saturday." Nicki said.

"It was nice meeting you, too." I said.

"Thank you for paying for my meal. I owe you one. You're a lifesaver, but we're going home. I'll hit you up tomorrow, Jamaican King" Star said and gave me a hug.

"Goodnight, beautiful. I'll talk to you later." I said.

Everyone got in their cars and left. Trey was making his way to me. I got a text from Kendra.

It was a picture of her bending over, showing her ass. I texted her back, "you should pick me up at my place so I can shower and spend the night over there. After that, I can make it to the interview." I said.

"They were pretty chill, huh. The Alpha girls were all fine as hell, but let's go home." Trey said.

"Yeah, they were. Star was nice herself. I can't wait to go to Chicago for this beach party." I said.

Beep, I saw I got a text from Kendra, asking for a picture. She wanted to know what I was wearing.

"Hey Trey, can you take a pic of me?" I asked.

"Sure. I got you and put it on Instagram, too. You don't have many pictures, haha. It gets your followers up. People will want to know who you are and how to find you." Trey said.

Trey took the picture of me and I sent it to Kendra. We got in the Jeep and headed home. When we went home, Trey went to his room and went to bed. I got undressed and got ready to take shower. Then I got a text from Kendra

"Wow, sexy ass hell. I'll be at your place in 10 mins. Make sure to pack your clothes so I can drop you off at your interview." Kendra said with a smiley face.

I took a shower, brushed my teeth and washed my face. I got dressed and put cologne on. I wanted to smell good for Kendra. When I checked my phone, she said she's here. I got my clothes packed in my new ISU book-bag. Left out of my apartment and got in Kendra's car.

"Wow, you smell very good, what's the name of it?" Kendra asked.

"It's called island breeze." I said.

"Well, I love it and I see you got some swag. I bet the hoes were all over you in the club. I'm surprised you're coming to my place to get some and not anybody else's." Kendra said.

When she said that, I started thinking about Isabel and us having sex.

"Yeah, but I'd rather finish what we started. Gotta take her time." I said.

"Me too, Rude boy." Kendra said .

We got to her new apartment. It had to be about 15 mins away from my place. We went inside and it was nice. It looked like she got new furniture. Her couch was black and her kitchen table was black, too. The kitchen was close to the living room.

She also had a big screen TV. Her place was decked out. We then walked into her bedroom. She got a new bed, too. She had candles lit, no lights. The room smelled like roses and sweet candles.

"Your apartment is nice. Wow, this is better than your last apartment. I see you got a bigger bed, too. Look at you, a grown woman doing it big." I said with a smile.

"Yeah, I'm happy to get out of my last place, but let me get ready for you." Kendra said in a sexy, slow voice.

She went inside her bathroom. I just looked around and got my condoms ready. I saw some honey on her night stand. I just started thinking of ideas of what to do with the honey, ideas that I always wanted to try.

"You like, rude boy?" Kendra asked.

She came out, wearing long black pantyhose with straps on them and a black bra to match. My dick got hard once I saw her in it.

"Yes, I love it. What do you have on? Come closer so I can see what you're wearing." I said.

She came closer with a slow sexy walk. Her long, curly hair was on her shoulders, touching her skin. It looked soft. I took my shirt off. She came to me and started rubbing my abs and licking them as well.

"I just love your body, rude boy. I want to lick honey off your abs down to your dick and play a game as well." Kendra said in a sexy voice.

I was thinking to myself, "Damn ,this mixed breed woman is freaky."

"Here, before we play the game. Take three shots of Tequila with me." Kendra said.

We took shots. I did two more. I don't like when people out drink with me. I wanted to get loose.

"Ok, about the game. We're going to take turns licking this honey off each other. I want us to take our time with our bodies. Feel each other and learn from each other, so sit back and lay on my bed." Kendra said.

When she said all this, I wanted to do anything she wanted to do and I was ready.

So I laid down as my dreads and back were laying on her pillow. My dick was poking out of my grey ISU cut off shorts. She pulled my shorts off. I was naked as she then poured honey on my abs to my dick. The honey wasn't cold. It was room temperature. After the honey was poured down, her face got close to my abs as she licked the honey off slowly. The honey was like a path to my dick and her tongue followed that path. Her tongue licked all around my hard dick. I felt her warm mouth as she moaned while sucking the honey off my tip. I looked at her and said, "my turn. I want you to put your face on the pillow and put your ass up in the air for me." I said.

She did what I said. I did put the honey on her lower back down to her ass hole. I licked the honey off her lower back. It was all gone. My tongue followed the honey trail to her ass crack down to the asshole. I licked clean around her asshole, clockwise and counterclockwise. She moaned, grabbed my head and told me to keep going. She said she never had her ass licked before. She moaned more and more. I kept eating her ass. I got down to the pussy and ate that as well. I took long licks to the asshole down to the pussy. She moaned and said, "Rudeboy, keep going please." I grabbed her titties and massaged her nipples while licking her ass. She told me she was cuming from me by just eating her ass alone. I kept licking around her asshole like I would do an ice cream cone. She came when my tongue made it to her pussy. She moaned louder, then I poured more honey around the rim of her asshole and used my finger to smear it around. I told her to suck my finger to get the honey off. She sucked the honey off like she did my dick. Then, I used both my big hands to pick her ass up. While I had my knees on the bed and her legs weren't touching the bed as I ate every last drop of honey around the rim of her ass. I moaned while doing it. She moaned more and more.

"Yes, rudeboy. Keep licking right there. Please don't stop." Kendra moaned.

I stopped licking her ass and told her to ride my face like a horse. Pick up my dreadlocks and use them as a rope halter.

"Pull my dreads hard if you want me to lick faster. Just pretend I'm a horse while you ride my face." I said.

"Wow, you're a super freak, but let's do it. Sounds different and sexy." Kendra said.

I laid my back on the bed while she climbed on top of a dark strong body and put her pussy on my face. She started going back and forth. She put my dreads in her hands as well. I licked around her pussy and she started moaning. She started riding my face faster and pulling my locks so I could lick faster.

"Yes rude boy, damn that feels so good. I'm about to cum again shit, you're so good." Kendra moaned.

I licked faster and my dick was hard. It was so hard, it was slapping against my abs while she was riding my tongue. She moaned and I moaned. She pulled my dreads harder as my tongue was going faster.

"I'm cumming. Yes, I'm cumming, baby!" Kendra moaned.

She screamed and came all over my face. She got off. I licked the juices around my lips and told her it was my turn.

"Yes, it is. Do what you want to me." Kendra said.

I got off the bed and put a condom on and rolled it down my dick.

"Lay on your stomach." I said.

She laid on her stomach. I got on top of her and went inside her. She moaned and grabbed the cover. I started giving her love strokes. I wasn't going fast at all, just rolling my dick inside her clockwise. I licked around her ear as she put her hand in my dreads and pulled and told me to go faster. So, I went fast as her ass cheeks were big under me. The bed was shaking and squeaking. I moaned and cussed in her ear. She bounced her ass on me while I bounced on her. I couldn't hold back.

"Yes, cum rude boy, cum for me. Hurry up, baby! Cum on my ass cheeks!" Kendra moaned.

Once she said that, I couldn't hold back.

I pulled out and took the condom off. I came all over her ass cheeks.

"Damn, that was good. Sorry I didn't know I was going to cum that much on you." I said, trying to catch my breath.

"It's ok. Them big balls of yours are carrying a lot, so I didn't expect anything little to get on me." She said,

She took her finger, dipped her finger on the nut on her butt and licked it off.

"You don't taste that bad either." Kendra said.

She went into the bathroom to clean herself and I did as well. We both laid down, cuddled and fell asleep

"Raise and Shine. It's time to get ready for your interview. You don't want to be late." Kendra said.

I started getting up. I struggled for a little bit and was kind of tired still, but I also smelled breakfast was getting cooked as well.

"I also cooked bacon and egg sandwiches. I don't want

you to go to your interview hungry." Kendra said in a caring way.

"Thank you. I guess I can get dressed. You don't mind if I shower, right?" I asked.

"Sure, go shower. I don't mind." Kenda said.

I got in the shower and am still trying to get up. I finished showering, got my clothes out of my book bag and got dressed. I put on a black polo, black shorts and black Nike's. I sprayed cologne on and made sure I put cocoa butter on my skin. I put on my golf watch as I went to the kitchen to eat.

"You look nice and smell good, I see. Showing them big ole arms, you're going to get a lot of women clients. Watch and see." Kendra said.

"Yeah, I have to see about that. The sun is nice and bright this morning, so it's going to be a good day." I said.

"Yes, it is. Here, eat your breakfast with your freaky ass. I've never had sex like that before. It was different, that's for sure, but amazing as well. You're this young and your sex game is this good? Mmmhmmm." Kendra said.

"Well, I do my best to please." I said.

I started eating breakfast and once I was finished, we left. She went to drop me off at the gym. It actually wasn't that far from my apartment.

"Thanks for the ride and breakfast. I had a great time, but I can walk home after the interview. It's a great day outside, plus it isn't that far." I said.

"Alright, let me know if you get the job, Ok? I'll talk to you later, rudeboy." Kendra said.

I looked outside of the gym. It was a nice size and the words, "Your Fitness" in big letters. I walked inside and the front desk was there.

"Hello, how may I help you?" The front desk lady asked.

"I have an interview with Jasmine at 9am." I said.

"Sure, I'll go get her." The front desk lady said.

I waited and I saw this pretty brown skin slim thick girl come out, wearing glasses.

"Hey, how are you doing? You must be Eason. I'm Jasmine." Jasmine said.

"Nice to meet you" as we shook hands.

"Follow me to my office."

While following to her office, she was wearing black yoga pants and a black 'Your Fitness' V neck. She had two tattoo sleeve arms, covered with beautiful tattoos with roses and other artwork. She looked like she could be a model for sure. We went inside her office and sat down. She sat behind her desk and I sat in front of her desk.

"So, Kendra told me you're looking to be a personal trainer. I see you have the body, that's for sure and you moved here from Jamaica." Jasmine said.

"Yes, I moved here to play soccer. I got a full scholarship." I said.

"You looked like a football player, but soccer it's cool. A lot of cardio in that sport. So what makes you a good personal trainer? A lot of clients here are women, so why should I hire you?"

"Well, I love fitness and I workout everyday. I know I can take my time with a woman's body when it comes to fitness goals. Every woman deserves to feel confident and sexy." I said.

"Yasssss. I mean, yes you're right about that. Well, the job is part time so you might work 2 to 3 days a week and I will pay you $15 per hour, plus commission when you sign clients. Also, you pretty much choose your hours, too." She explained.

I kept looking at her body while she was sitting down. She had long, straight hair, too. Her smile was nice.. I saw that she had trophies and medals around the office too.

"Well, congratulations! The job is yours! I'll text you everything as well and what time you will start." she said.

"So I see you're in great shape as well. You ran track, I see. Must have been good." I said.

"Yeah, I used to run track at ISU. Ran for 4 seasons and placed at nationals, too. I placed 3rd right now. I box to keep in shape." Jasmine said.

"Yeah, I can see the muscles you have. I'm thinking about running track as well after my soccer season." I said.

"Oh, really. What event do you want to run?" Jasmine asked.

"The 400 in 100 meter. I can run fast for a long time. I have great endurance and speed for the 100 meter." I said.

"I ran the 100 meter in the 200 myself. I'm going to have to see how fast you are. I know how strong you are." Jasmine said in a sneaky voice.

"How do you know that?" I asked.

"I seen your video on Instagram and you're strong as hell. I am pretty sure that's a record and don't be surprised if the coaches ask you to play football." Jasmine said.

"That's a no. I'm going pro after one season." I said.

" You're that good, huh. One of the trainers here, she's a soccer player. This is her last season, coming up, then she's going pro as well."

"I'm going to have to meet her then." I said.

"You will. Well, I have to get back to work. I will talk to you later." Jasmine said.

She walked me out of the gym. While walking me out, I saw that sexy curvy BBW who I saw at the mall. We both looked at each other. I got the memories of her body and face I needed because I was going to go home in jack off. I left the gym, started walking home and I remember I wanted to get my dreads done, so I texted Nisha. "How are you doing? This is Eason." It was 9:45 A.M. She called me.

"Hey Eason, this is the Jamaican brother from the mall, right?" Nisha asked.

"Yes, it's me. I wanted to get my dreads done today if you got time." I said.

"Yes, I called because I think I saw you walking out of Your Fitness gym." Nisha said.

"Yeah, I just came out of an interview." I said.

"Well, the interview went well, but I'm on my way to the salon. You can be my first head today if that's cool?" Nisha said.

"Sure, I would love that."

"You want a ride? I'm on my way there now." Nisha said.

"Sure." I said.

"Alright, look behind you. I am in the black dodge." She said.

I looked behind me and it was her. So I got in the car.

"I guess I got here just in time, looking sexy and what not." Nisha said.

"Why thank you, you're looking sexy as well, wearing my country colors." I said.

"Yeah, I love the colors, so what type of job do you get at the gym?" Nisha asked.

"A personal trainer. Making some money while I'm out here, you know." I said.

"I understand that. Here, let's go. I'm actually not that far from your school."

So we drove off and started driving to her salon. I checked my phone, I saw that a video was sent to me it was Isabel and I having sex. My phone was loud. Nisha saw and heard it.

"Wow, I see you were going down on shawty ass, huh." Nisha said with a laugh.

"Sorry about that, I didn't know she recorded us and she just sent this video of me." I said, feeling embarrassed.

"Don't be. It looks like she's loving it and I see y'all were doing my favorite position, too. Shawty got some ass on here too." Nisha said with a smile.

"Yeah, she does." I said.

I texted her back, saying I didn't know you recorded us.

"Well, we are here at my salon. It's called Nisha Hair. You're going to love what I do to your hair." Nisha said.

We got out of the car and she was looking sexy and curvy. She was wearing sandals to show her pretty feet. Her toenails were green as well. Her fingernails were green and white and her pants were black. Her shirt was yellow and green. We walked in the salon and it was nice. She had 6 salon chairs. I saw sinks where women get their hair washed and saw a table with magazines on them. Also a black couch and chairs. Everything else were black, too. Even the sinks. Each hair station had big mirrors, too.

"This is nice. How long have you been open for business?" I asked.

"About a year now. I moved here from Saint Louis about 4 years ago. I followed my ex boyfriend here. When I followed him here, I found out he was cheating on me and left me." Nisha said.

"Sorry about that, but the woman he left you for has to deal with the problem, not you." I said.

"Well, he didn't cheat on me with a woman, he cheated on me and left me for a man. I walked in from work, hearing moaning I'm thinking it's a bitch he's fucking on, but naw, it was a man, fucking him. If it would had been a woman, I would had maybe stayed, maybe work it out, but a women I can't compete with no nigga, so I broke it off with him. He then moved down to Atlanta with his lover and I haven't heard from him since." Nisha said.

"That's crazy and wild. I'm sorry you had to go through such pain, but hey, look at you now. You look happy. You have a beautiful salon. How did you get started in the business anyway?" I asked.

"Well, I used to work at a gas station and I hated it, but I did hair on the side and was pretty good at it. A few of my clients told me I should go into business for myself, but that kind of thing takes money. So I was looking for ways to make money, then one day, this truck driver came to my job. He would get gas time by time. One day, he came in wearing normal clothes, but he was dressed nicely and I saw a nice BMW I8. I asked him questions about how much money I can make as a truck driver and he told me everything. So once he told me $1,500 to $7,500 a week or more, I said fuck it and got my CDLs. Two months after that, I got the job and went over the road for two years to save my money to have that salon I wanted and the rest was history." Nisha said.

"That's amazing. I would never think of a woman truck driver. I've never seen one before, but you were hungry. You got what you wanted." I said.

"Yeah, dreams come true, my Jamaican friend. I have five people working under me. My plan in the next five years is to have another Nisha hair salon open up in Saint Louis." Nisha said with passion.

"I love that idea." I said.

"Well, let's go wash your hair. Have a seat over here at the wash station." Nisan told me.

I went to the wash station and I took my polo off so I wouldn't get it wet.

"I see that you're cut up with their abs too. Can I touch them please?" Nisan asked.

"Sure."

She put both of her hands on my abs and rubbed them.

"Wow, they are hard, I see. You can use them as an iron board. Let me stop before my old ass gets in trouble, touching on a young man like you." Nisha said.

"You're good. I know how to keep a secret and the last time I checked, I'm of age." I said in a sexy clam voice.

We both looked at each other and there was some sexual

tension.

"Whatever. I'm 35 years old, so stop it. Sit down here and lay your head back so I can wash these beautiful locks." Nisha said.

I sat down and put my head back on the sink. She put a towel over my chest and turned the water on. She took these mini water holes out to wash my hair in it. It was a part of the sink. She sprayed the water on my locs, all over my locs too. They got wet, then she got some shampoo and poured a lot in her hand. Rubbed her hands together to massage it in my head. The shampoo smelled good and her massage felt good. I closed my eyes to enjoy the massage.

"That feels really good. I never had this done before." I said.

"Yeah, I have blessed hands. They like to tell me." Nisha said.

She got more shampoo and rubbed it in my head some more. Her fingers felt perfect while washing my hair. Her big breasts were all over my face, I wanted to lick them. Her breasts had green glitter on them. When she moved, her titties moved. I couldn't help but get hard by looking at them and getting a massage. My dick was jumping out my shorts like it wanted to grab her.

"So tell me about Jamaica. I heard that it's a party island. But it has poor parts as well, like some really poor parts." Nisha was saying.

"Yes, I actually grew up in such poor parts, but I'm fortunate to have a better life now." I said.

"Wow, that's crazy. I don't know how someone could live like that. Sleeping on floors and not really having a home, like a real house... I saw people using old scrap metal and wood for a home. I saw kids missing meals. Just a sad way to live for anyone." Nisha said.

"Yeah, that's why when I go pro, I'm going to give back to my community. Build homes and put money in jobs there as well. No one shouldn't go hungry. I will change that." I said in a serious voice.

"I know that's right. You're a good man that you are going to help your people." Nisha said.

"Yeah, I feel like God blessed me to do so like Moses." I said.

"I know that's right. A strong man with goals and speaking strongly, that snake in your pants needs to be put away. I saw it jumping at me too." Nisha said.

"Sorry about that, you had nice big ole tits in my face and your hands felt good. I couldn't help it, plus you being a sexy boss woman is a turn on itself, you know." I said while looking into her eyes.

"You better stop looking at me with those piercing green eyes you got before they get you in trouble. Here, follow me to the dryer." Nisha said while looking me up and down.

So I followed her to the dryer while looking at her water balloon booty shake.

"Sit here. Once your hair is dry, I'm going to braid them and line you up." Nisha said.

So I sat down and waited for my hair to dry.

"I'll be right back." Nisha said.

I watched her lock the door and walk to the back. I texted Isabel and said 'I didn't know you took a video of us'. She text backed, saying she was sorry and did it because she wanted to masturbate to our sex. "I masturbated to our sex twice this morning." She texted. My dick started to get hard again and I watched the video a bit as well. It was sexy and she was riding my dick on the couch, doing the reverse cowgirl position. I put my hand on top of my dick to push it down.

"Your hair might be done now. It's been about 30 minutes. Let me see if it's dry." Nisha said.

She came over and left the dryer above my head and started feeling on my locs.

"Yes, they are dry I see. That's good. Let's get started." Nisha said.

So I followed her and watched her ass again.

"I see you looking at my ass." Nisha said.

"How did you know that?" I asked.

She pointed at a mirror and smiled.

"You got caught, it's cool though. Now sit here so I can get started on your braids." Nisha said.

I sat down at her station and she started braiding my dreads. They started to get tight with each braid.

"I'm going to braid four nice sized braids. You're going to love it and they will last a long time too." Nisha said.

"So, tell me about your family?" I asked.

"My family ain't shit, to be honest. They only call when they want money. I remember it was a time when I didn't have a dime to my name and I needed help badly, but they didn't do shit for me. I told myself okay I will remember that and when I come up, don't ask me for a dime. Years later, now I'm the one with money in my family and they ask me for money. I tell them nope and they get mad. I also own three houses, while I rent from a condo right now." Nisha said.

"Why is that when you can own a home?" I asked.

"Because I don't see myself living here forever or starting a family. But I knew I would be here for a while, so I got into the real estate game and saw some houses for cheap. I knew I could fix them up and rent them out, so I did. I am all about growing my money and having it work for me, so I don't need another person for money again." Nisha said.

"I can understand that. Sad how people can be, but when I get my money soon in the future, you can help me buy houses to rent out." I said.

"I can do that handsome."

We talked more about *business*. I was learning things I didn't know about real estate. She was a smart woman and I loved the convo.

"While I'm done braiding your hair, let me line you up now. Took me about an hour and a half, but I got it done." Nisha said.

She started lining my head up. I've never had my hair lined before.

"I'm done. Here, let me spray your hair and here is a mirror." Nisha said while giving me a hand mirror.

I took the mirror and I loved what I saw. The locs were braided tight and the line was sharp and perfect.

"Wow, you did an amazing job. You got me feeling confident and sexy to be honest." I said with a smile.

"You're right, you do look sexy. This hairstyle is very nice on you."

"How much do I owe you?" I asked.

"Just give me $85." She said.

"I gave her 100 and told her to keep the change." I said.

"Thanks, I appreciate it. Let me show you around the shop more." Nisha said.

We walked to the back, I got closer to her booty and bumped against her.

"Excuse me, I didn't mean to." I said.

"It's cool." Nisha said with a smile.

She pushed her booty back on me. I got hard and I held her from the back so she could feel that I was hard.

"Yeah, you're trying to get in trouble, huh? Mmm I got a little time. Here, follow me back here." Nisha said in a sexy voice.

I followed her to the back room, we started kissing and feeling each other. I pulled my shorts down, she pulled this chair up and sat down. Then, she pulled me closer and started sucking my dick.

"Mmm this chocolate big dick tastes good, too. I'm going to enjoy this." Nisha said.

She rubbed my balls while sucking my dick and made this washing machine noise while my dick was in her mouth. It felt warm and good at the same time. She put her tongue in my pee hole. That's when I started moaning. I've never felt any head like this before. She started licking my balls fast and jacking me at the same time. After that, she started moaning while sucking my dick again.

"I told you to leave me alone before you get in trouble." Nisha said while sucking my dick.

I moaned and was trying my best not to cum, but she started sucking my dick, making that washing machine sound again and I told her I was cumming. She went faster and faster. I came hard in her mouth. She swallowed my nut like a strawberry soda and she started sucking my dick like a straw, trying to suck the rest of the nut out of my dick. She had me speechless.

"I told you to stop, I see your dick is still hard." Nisha said in a sexy, confident voice.

"Yes. To be honest, that was the best head I've ever had in my life." I said in a surprised voice.

"Yeah, I've heard that before, that's why I took a seat. Why are you still hard, mmm you have a condom?" Nisha asked.

"Yes I do. Bend over here. Put your knees on this chair." I said.

She pulled her pants down and all this ass just fell out of the pants. It was a lovely sight. Her ass was brown and big. She put her knees on the chair. I pulled the condom out of my pocket and smacked my dick on her ass cheeks. It looked like a wave with each smack on the ass check. I rolled the condom down my dick and went inside, starting out fast.

"Yasss Eason, mmmmm that feels so good. Hurry up, my employees will be here soon." Nisha moaned.

So I went faster and put both my hands around her small waist and her ass started moving like a mad ocean. As I moaned, she moaned too.

"Shit! God damn this some good ass dick! I'm about to cum! Go faster, please go faster!" Nisha moaned.

So I went faster, trying to hold my cum back again.

"I'm cumming! Yasss I'm cumming right now shittttt

mmmmmmmmm!" Nisha moaned

When she started cumming, I started cumming too.

"Damn, that was good. I guess what I heard about Jamaican and it is sex is true. I haven't had good back shots that good in years. Usually people don't last long back there." Nisha said with a smile.

"Trust me, I almost tapped out, but damn, your sex is great. I love how your wrist is small and you're so thick." I said.

"Yeah, it's genes. My mom and grandma are built this way too." Nisha said.

"I see, I love it." I said.

She pulled her pants up and walked over to me. Pulled my condom off that was full of cum and cleaned my dick and balls for me. She did it slowly and softly so that I almost got hard again. When she was done, she grabbed my dick and kissed it.. She threw the condom away.

"I see we had some sexual tension built up between us." Nisha said.

"Yes, I agree. We're going to have to meet again." I said.

"Hello? Anyone here? Nisha, where are you?!" We heard a voice and made sure we looked normal like we didn't just had sex. We walked out to the front.

"Hey girl, this is my new client, Eason. I was just showing him around the shop." Nisha said.

"Oh, you did his dreads? They are very nice. My name is Sandra by the way. You must play football at ISU."

"It's nice to meet you and nope. I'm a soccer player." I said to Sandra.

"You have an accent, I see. You must be Jamaican. I know that accent when I hear it." Sandra said.

"Yes I am, you must have been there before?" I asked.

"Yes, I have a lot of times. My sisters and I used to go there a lot to party in the summer."

Ring ring

"It was my phone. Well, it was nice to meet you." Sandra said.

"Well, I should be going. I'll talk to you later, Nisha" I said.

"Alright take care."

We both looked at each other as our energy and bodies didn't want to leave each other. We smiled at each other and I left. I saw that I actually wasn't far from my apartment, so I just walked home. When I got home, I opened the door and saw Trey in the kitchen.

"What you up to dawg and damn, I see you got your dreads done. That shit looks nice ass hell." Trey said.

"Yeah, I went to Nisha after my interview at 'Your Fitness'." I said.

"Yeah she did good by you. I need to go by there and get ole girl to cut my hair soon, but I was actually leaving to get my chest tattoo. You want to come with? I know you said you wanted to get tatted." Trey asked.

"Yes sure, let me get some money." I said.

I went in my room and took out some money and changed my clothes into ISU clothing my coach gave me.

"Alright bet, let's go. It's not that far from here, so we can just walk there." Trey said.

So I followed Trey and we left our apartment.

CHAPTER 5

"What tattoos are you thinking about getting?" Trey asked.

"I want a tattoo sleeve. I want a tribal on my chest, half way arm. Then on my forearm, prayer hands with clouds and wings around it." I said.

"Damn, that sounds nice. I see that you're going all the way in on your first tattoo. They actually have good deals, too. And, they work fast. You might get all that done in 6 hours. People on campus were telling me about this place, so it's my first time coming here too." Trey said.

We kept walking and we made it to the tattoo shop. The name of it was 'Jessica Tattoo's shop.' We walked in. I saw two white girls and a mixed girl, covered in tattoos. One was tall and a pretty BBW, but her neck was covered with tats. The other girl was average height, decent size, wearing gauges in her ears. She also had tattoos all over her and her neck. She had pink hair, then the mixed girl was thick and pretty with long two braids. She had tattoo sleeves and her upper back was tatted as well. The tattoo shop on the inside was pink and black with a big trophy case on the wall with a lot of trophies inside. It also had photos of the mixed girl in a woman biker gang with a pink and black motorcycle.

"How may I help you guys? I'm Jessica by the way." she said.

"Hey, my name is Trey. I called in earlier to set up an appointment. I think her name was Summer." Trey said.

"Hi, I'm Summer. Yes, we did talk. Come over here. I'll get you set up." Summer said.

Summer was the tall BBW. She had a big wide booty and the way she was smiling at Trey, I'm pretty sure he could get more than tattoos.

"And what's your name, green eyes?" Jessica asked with a smile.

"I'm Eason. I'm here to get tattooed as well." I said.

"Well, I'm free and tell me what tattoos you want." Jessica said.

"I would love to get a tribal tattoo. I want the tattoo to be on my chest, bicep, my shoulders and my forearm. I want prayer hands with clouds and wings around the hands. I want the hands to be holding a Rosary." I explained.

"Wow, that's going to be sexy. Ok, I can do all that. Come to my station and take your shirt off." Jessica said.

I went over to her station and took my shirt off. I sat on the chair.

"So where are you from with that accent? I might as well get to know you because we're going to be sitting here for about

6 hours. It's 2:05pm now. We should be done around 8 P.M." Jessica said.

"I am from Jamaica." I said.

"Nice. That's different from what I've seen around these parts. I also love your dreads locs and I love how they are braided," Jessica said.

"Thank you. I just had them done today. I love your braids. They fit you well." I said while looking at her hair.

"Thanks handsome. You will be my first Jamaican client." Jessica said with a smile.

"Well, that's good. I also love how you got the tattoo shop set up. It's different. I have never been in a woman tattoo shop before. I see that you have a lot of trophies and I see that you have pictures with some famous people. Do you travel? That's good." I said.

"Yeah, I entered a lot of tattoo contests in the past five years. I travel all over to show my talents. I'm going to draw up a nice design for you. You should love it." Jessica said to me with a smile.

"So tell me. How did you get into the tattoo business." I asked.

"Well, I grew up in a super religious home. I couldn't have a boyfriend and listen to any Hip-Hop because the lyrics were bad. I had friends who didn't go to church and had no guy friends at all. I couldn't watch what I wanted to watch at all because it might have sex or cussing in it. I couldn't go to sleepovers or parties at all. I wanted to be a dancer or an artist because I'm actually good at both, but my parents said that isn't God's work at all. So they wanted me to go to these Christian Colleges in the middle of nowhere in Iowa with all girls only." She said.

"So did you go?" I asked.

"Nope. I said fuck that shit. They already fucked up my childhood. I wasn't going to let them mess up my adulthood. When I graduated high school and turned 18. I told them I wasn't going to that college. They were pissed, they told me to move out and never come back because I'm the Devil's Daughter. That's why I got Devil's Daughter tattooed on my upper back." Jessica said while showing me her tattoo. It was sexy in red and black letters.

"That's crazy and that's actually a nice tattoo. I know your parents wouldn't like it at all." I said.

"Fuck no. They hate tattoos on people. They used to call it the Devil's markings." Jessica said while going about drawing my tattoo.

"So, what happened next when you moved out?" I asked.

"Well, when they kicked me out haha. My cousin in Atlanta GA said I could live with her, so I took the greyhound with my book bag of clothes and headed down there. My parents hated her because she did what she wanted, but I loved her for that. It was different and she seemed free of rules. I was a slave to a religion and she was free to the world. She was free in my eyes, but when I went to Atlanta, she picked me up in a white Range Rover. I have the same one outside, but mine is pink and black because when I saw hers, I told myself I was going to get one too. Her apartment was laid out with nice designer clothes. She was doing her thang and she was the same age as me. She was independent. I asked her what her job was and how she could afford such a nice apartment and a nice ride. She told me she was a stripper. She worked at this club called Magic City. I was a good dancer and wanted to make money. So I said fuck it, I'll do it too. I started working the first night I got there and I was nervous, not going to lie, but I took some shots of watermelon ciroc and that night, I showed the world my body and dancing skills.

"How did you do?" I asked while enjoying the story.

"Did good. I made 500 dollars that night and made 2,100 that week in due time. I got my own place. I ended up going to an art school while being a stripper. Art was my passion too. I got into making tattoos. I practiced on my cousin. At first, I sucked. Then, I got a lot better over time. I started tattooing the other strippers and rappers too. I started making more money doing tattoos than stripping, so I retired from stripping. Those were fun days though. I knew I couldn't do it forever, so I used the stripper money I saved up in two years and paid for a tattoo shop that I also own in Atlanta. This is my 2nd one and, I'm going to open more in due time." Jessica said.

"Wow, I love your story. I'm happy that you're doing what you're passionate about. It's sad that your parents were that selfish, but you're happy at the end of the day." I said.

"Yes I am, I mean of course I miss them. I know if they see me again like this, they would judge me and to be honest, they haven't called me or anything once they found out I became a stripper and got into tattoos." Jessica said with a disappointed face.

"Well, maybe in the future they will stop judging and be your parents." I said.

"Yeah. Maybe so. Well, I'm done drawing. It's time for me to be your first. Here, I'm going to rub this drawing on you where I'm going to tattoo it." Jessica said.

She rubbed the paper on me with the drawing while she's going to tattoo me at. I was a little scared, but I wanted it done. Her hands also touched my skin while doing it and I was enjoying it. She looked in my eyes and I looked into hers. She took the tattoo gun out and turned it on.

"Alright, I'm about to start. No holding back." Jessica said.

I looked at her and said "I'm ready" and I closed my eyes waiting for her to start.

I felt a little pitch, but not bad at all. I opened my eyes and she was tattooing me. It wasn't painful at all.

"It isn't that bad, I thought it was going to hurt." I said, feeling relief.

"Yeah, some people can't take the pain, some just don't mind the pain." Jessica said.

"So, are you single? I know a beautiful intelligent woman like you got a man." I asked, hoping she would say no.

"No, I'm actually single. I had a man about a year ago, but he cheated on me with my cousin who I was telling you about." Jessica said.

"I didn't see that coming at all. I thought y'all were best friends." I said with a surprised face.

"Me too. I couldn't get a hold of my cousin or my ex one night, but his brother Facebook messaged me saying my man was cheating on me with my cousin right now at my cousin's house. I told him to call me ASAP and I gave him my number. He called me, telling me that they have been fucking each other for awhile now, so I drove over there and I saw his car parked a block away. That shit didn't work." Jessica said.

"So, what happened next?" I asked.

"Well, I went to the back window and I saw them fucking. My heart was crushed and I started crying. Hearing her moan and him saying that was the best pussy he ever had crushed my soul. My world just dropped. I got mad and wanted them to feel my pain too. So I recorded it just in case they try to play dumb ass fuck and I left I let them finish." Jessica said with a smile.

"Why would you do that? I would have broken in and

started acting like a crazy man." I said.

"Because I had a plan and I wanted to hurt them back, so that night I called his brother. I knew he had a thing for me and was looking out for me, so I went over his brother house and recorded us having sex. I told his brother this is the best dick I ever had in my life and that you're way better and bigger than your bum ass brother. I sucked his dick too and made sure he came all over my face and ass cheeks to kill my ex's soul. Then, for my slut ass cousin, I told her baby daddy that she was dating. He didn't believe me and I showed him the video. He was pissed. Her baby was handsome but I just told him. So we had sex too and I recorded that as well." Jessica said.

"Damn, this story is getting sexy, but good at the same time. I'm kind of getting turned on. You're a bad Girl, but what happened next?" I said while watching her tattoo my chest.

"Haha, you're funny I see. So I got them all in one room at my place. I lied and said we were having a get together. My slut ass cousin was there with her man, feeling good about life and my man was there too. I saw them smile at each other. It pissed me off so I said to everybody "I got this new movie. It's pretty cool. It's called Back Stabbing. Here, I'm about to play it," so I played my cousin and my ex's video of them, having sex. They looked at each other and looked at me, saying sorry and they messed up and to forgive them all of that weak shit because they got caught. Her baby daddy was pissed. He told me to play the other video. It's called revenge. So I played it and they saw us having sex. My cousin's face dropped and she got pissed calling me names. Then, I played another video for my ex. He thought he was off the hook. Naw nigga, your turn to hurt and I played the video of me fucking his brother. Long story short, we all were fighting, haha." Jessica said while laughing.

"Damn, that would hurt me. I'm pretty sure they are still hurt from that, that was good revenge." I said.

"Yeah, because my cousin has to see her baby daddy and have to deal with him. My ex has to deal with his brother. I wanted to make a statement so I did, don't fuck me over." Jessica said with a serious face.

"Trust me, I know not to get on your bad side." I said.

We finished talking. She told more about her dreams and I told her about mine. She loved my idea about having my own weed farm and that she wanted to be part of it when I got started. We talked about each other's bodies. She loved my abs and I told her I loved her thick legs. She gave me her number and I gave her mine. I told her maybe we could hang out tonight to enjoy each other's company. She said maybe, just text me. I took a nap and I fell asleep.

"Wake up sleepy head, I am finished with your tattoo." Jessica said while shaking me to wake up.

I got up, checked the time and it was 8:15 pm. I saw it was dark outside. I saw my tattoo was finished. It looked amazing.

The tribal was big and very detailed, just like my forearm tattoo. It was connected just right. She did a great job. I saw that Trey was gone and the other girls were gone too.

"So, do you like it?" She asked.

"No, I love it. You did an amazing job. I want to hug you but it kind of hurts a bit, haha." I said,

"Well, maybe you can hug me later over some drinks at my place. Maybe not tonight, but I'll let you know, I'll cook us some dinner too." Jessica said.

"Well, I would love that. Where is Trey and the other girls?" I asked.

"Trey been done. He saw you were asleep and didn't want to wake you up. And, my employees left to get us food." Jessica said.

"Alright, this tattoo is nice though. I hope it heals nicely." I said.

"Yes, it will heal nicely. Just put this cream on it. Here, let me rub this healing cream." Jessica said while getting the cream and putting it in her hands.

She put the cream on the tattoos. It feels good. She was rubbing me down slowly and she messaged the cream on me. It felt so good, I got hard. She went down to my hand.

"Wow, your hands are big. I see you have big feet too. What size you wear and what's your height, tall self." Jessica asked while looking me up and down as she was still rubbing the cream on me.

"I wear a size 14 and I am 6'4 ft tall." I said.

"I see that you're strong too. Let me stop before I get in trouble. Come with me so I can check you out." Jessica said.

I followed her to the cashier and he told me it was 400 dollars. I gave her 400 dollars, then the girls and Trey came in.

"Dawg, that tattoo is fire. She did her thang with this one." Trey said while looking at the tattoo.

"Yes she did. It fits your muscles too. These hoes all over campus are going to be all over you I'll tell you. My name is Kattie." Kattie said.

"Yes, it's nice. I love it. Jessica did her thing with you and my name is Monica. I go to ISU too. This is my last year at the school." Monica said.

"Here, I got some BBG shirts and also follow my Instagram @BBG_SelfMade. If your friends ask, they can order them there." Trey said while handing the shirts to girls.

"These are cute!!! Plus, I see you got my favorite colors, pink and black. Just bring me some more. If not, a box full and I will pass these out with your business cards to help get your followers up. I'll even give some to strippers too, around ATL," Jessica said.

"Thank you, that will really help me out." Trey said.

"It's nice to meet y'all and I'll be seeing y'all again soon because I'm pretty sure I will want more tattoos." I said while getting ready to leave.

Trey and I left the shop. I still had my shirt off, letting my tattoo air dry. We started walking back home.

"The girls back there were pretty cool and they were fine. I seen you and Jessica were hitting it off." Trey said.

"Yeah, Jessica is sexy, but I saw you with the tall BBW. She likes you." I said with a smile.

"Yeah, she's coming over tonight. I like BBW women, plus she had a nice wide booty too.

"Yeah, she was thick and wasn't soppy either. I'm going to hang out with Jessica soon." I said.

"Oh yeah!!! One of the Alpha girls texted me the details of the beach party tomorrow. The party starts at noon, plus it's going to be nice and sunny in Chicago too." Trey said.

"I can't wait!!! I hope it's drinks and ganja there." I said.

"You know it will be, plus there will be BBQ too. We are about to eat, drink and smoke well." Trey said while giving me a hand clap.

I looked ahead and I saw two white boys and a asian boy walking to me and Trey.

"Are you Eason from Jamaica?" One of the white boys asked.

"Yes I am, how can I help you? I asked.

"We are on the soccer team too. We saw that video of you bench pressing 550 pounds. Man you have football power, plus you got the size I see. My name is Don by the way. This is my sophomore season coming up." Don said while shaking my hand and Trey's hand.

"It's nice to meet you. I heard great things about you. My name is Jake. This is my sophomore season as well." Jake said while shaking my hand and Trey's hand.

"My name is Lee. This is my freshman season like you. I'm from China, I'm foreign like you." Lee said while shaking my hand and Trey's hand.

"I am Trey. I play football here. I am Eason's roommate. It's nice to meet y'all." Trey said.

"Well, we came over because we are about to play soccer at the field tonight and wanted to see if you want to play some night soccer with us." Don said.

"Sure, I would love to. Let me go home and get my cleats. I'll meet you guys over there." I said.

"Cool. We'll see you then. We're about to start in 30 mins." Jake said.

Trey and I then started walking again back home, so I could get my things.

"Awww shit, I'm about to come and watch this shit. They just want to see what you're working with." Trey said.

"Yes, I know. Jake is the best one out of them. He's more

athletic" I said.

"How do you know that?" Trey asked with a confused look.

"Because I know an athlete when I see one." I said.

We made it to the apartment and I got my cleats and left to go to the field. The field wasn't far, Trey said while walking with me until we got there. I saw a lot of people there. I saw 20 people or more on the field and a lot of people on the sideline. It was a legit game. The field was beautiful. It had big red goalies on each side. The lights were bright and shining on the field. They were playing music while white girls and boys danced. It looked like people were warming up too. Getting ready to play, I got my Jamaica color cleats on and I was wearing a Jamaican white shirt that said "Jamaican Soccer." I also saw girls on the sideline looking at me and Trey.

"Man it's lit tonight here, y'all soccer players be out here deep I see. I see the soccer hoes here too, dancing. They're playing my song by Nav And Meek. 'A-hole, Uber on the way, hoe.' Yeah, it's lit" Trey said while rapping the song and moving to the beat.

"Yeah, it's a lot of people here, but I'm ready." I said while stretching my legs.

"Hey Eason, I see you made it. You're going to play with us. We are playing king of the field and we are up now to play." Jake said.

"Alright, I'm ready to go," I said.

I looked up, the lights were bright and I started walking on the field as I looked back. Some girls came, walking to him. I made it to the middle of the field.

"Alright Eason. It's me, Lee, Don and Zack. He's in the ISU team too." Jack said.

"Nice to Me you Eason, I heard great things about you." Zack said while shaking my hand.

"Right now, we are just doing 6 on 6. Our goalie is there. He's just a guy we picked up. The other team is actually from the community college, so let's show them that ISU is king of the field. It's 3 others teams that are waiting to play too, so let's show them up y'all Red birds on 3. One, two, three." Jake said.

"Redbirds!" We all yelled. A guy holding a mic started coming to us.

"Y'all got your team together, I see. Good. It's time to play. I'm going to be the referee and scorekeeper, but mainly the announcer on this fine night of soccer. Have fun and play safe." The Announcer said.

I huddled up with my team to ask what the scoring rules were.

"First one to 6 goals or when 15 mins hit on the time clock and whoever has more goals wins." Jack said.

The other team came to the middle of the field so we could begin to play. They were wearing yellow jerseys. I looked them up and down and tried to see who was their best player.

Alright, y'all ready to play? The yellow team was going to have the ball first before I blew the whistle. Is everybody ready??" The Announcer said while holding the cordless mic.

Both teams said they were ready and *The Announcer* blew the whistle so we could start the game. I saw the guy I wanted to guard didn't have the ball yet. The other team started kicking the ball to each other. I saw that in the other guy's eyes, he wanted to pass it to my guy, so I act like I was running somewhere else, then when he pass him the ball, I ran full speed and stole the ball away from him and ran full speed, started kicking the ball down the field so I can make a goal.

"Damn y'all see the wheels on this kid? He stole the ball fast as fuck. He's already down the field with the ball." The Announcer said while talking on the mic.

I saw one guy trying to catch up, then I stopped fast with the ball, using my feet to stop the ball. He then was running fast too, so I slowed down. He fell down and I kept running. I got to the goalie and I kicked the ball in fast and the goalie didn't block the ball. I made the first score.

"Goal!!!!!! Y'all see that move he just pulled to make him fall? He just scored that fast, man. Let's see what other moves he got." The Announcer said.

I saw Trey cheering me on.

"That's what I'm talking about nigga." Trey said while

jumping up and down.

Nice move and score my team said and we got back on defense. I started watching who had the ball and I knew he wanted to pass it to the game guy again because I had a feeling he was the best guy on the team. Then the guy I was guarding got the ball. He tried to pass it to someone else, but I stole it again and ran fast down the field while dribbling the ball with my feet. Three guys tried to run towards me, but Jake was open, so I kicked the ball over the heads to Jake and he then dribbled the ball down the field and kicked it back to me. I'm dribbling the ball full speed. They couldn't catch up to me and I got close to the goalie again and kicked it hard and fast. I made another goal. I started hearing cheering.

"Goal!!!!! This kid is the real deal. Another goal by him again. He has some serious wheels on him with great ball control. Red team 2 to 0." The announcer says in the mic.

"You're fast dude, I think I'm going to love playing with you." Don said.

The other teammates came to me and told me good job again. The other team started kicking the ball down the field and one of them said something to me.

"That shit is luck, bet you can't guard me." One of them said.

He got the ball as he tried to get past me, but I was all

over him. He then kicked it back to his teammate and his teammate kicked it to him again, then he tried to get past me and I stole the ball while dribbling the ball down the field, full speed again, out-running every one on the field, even my teammates. Got to their goalie and kicked it hard and fast again. I made the goal. My team then ran down to me, cheering me on. I saw Trey clapping his hands.

"Goal!!!!!!! 3 in a row. I hope he's playing soccer for ISU because they need this kid." the announcer said.

The other team came back, kicking the ball down the field again. I looked at Jack and he knew what I wanted to do. We then double team someone with the ball. I then stole the ball and ran full speed down the field again. I could have easily made another goal, but I wanted my teammates to make goals too. So I stopped and passed it to Lee and Lee was getting guarded as he passed it back to me. I passed it to jack. He was the goalie and he made the score. Jack ran up to me.

"Nice pass. Let's finish these fools so we can play the next team and kill them too." Jake said.

The other team got down the field and started passing it to each other, getting close to our goal. I ran to Jack and told him to get ready to run down the field. I'm about to steal it. He looked at me and shook his head. The yellow team kicked the ball a little closer to our goal area. I ran full speed to the person who had the ball and stole it. Jake started running full speed down the field. I kicked the ball all the way down to Jack. I ran full speed down the field. Jack kicked the ball to me while the ball was in the air. I did a bicycle kick to the goal and made the goal while landing with a back flip, not on my back and everyone on the field went crazy.

"Goal!!!!! He did a fucking Cristiano Ronaldo bicycle kick and landed that shit with a backflip. The score is 5-0 now. One more goal and It's over with. Man, this kid is amazing. I just got word he's from Jamaica and he's playing for ISU this season. I'm going to be at all the games, that's for sure. I got this shit recorded too." The Announcer said while talking on the mic.

"That was a great ass move. Dude, you need to be in the pros. I hate to say this, but college might be too easy for you. I know skill when I see it." Don said.

"Thanks man. Let's finish this game." I said.

We won the game 6 to 0. We also won every game we played. After we won 4 more games, we beat every team and people knew who I was now because I scored 3 to 4 goals in each game. I could have easily scored 6, but I didn't want to be greedy, so I made sure I didn't score all the goals.

"Man, it was nice playing with you. I can't wait to play with you this season. We are going to win a lot of games, that's for sure." Jake said.

"Why did you come here? It's like you're way too good to be playing college soccer to be honest. I'm sure you could have gone pro right after high school." Lee said in a curious way.

"Well, my plan is to go pro after this season to be honest. I was offered to play here and I have never been to America before. I wanted the college, experience you know." I said while we were walking off the field. I took my shirt off so I can cool down on this hot summer night.

"I can respect that. Well, we play here all the time. A lot of us aren't here for the summer, so we do this to keep in shape. If you're ever free, come out man. We'll love to play with you and to be honest, we never won King Of the field before, so thanks for that and see you later." Don said while walking off the field.

Everybody was excited and happy for me. People on the sideline came to talk to me and the ladies did too. Some stayed to finish playing, but I wanted to shower, eat and go home.

"Man, you were doing your thing out there. After seeing you kill it like that and seeing it with my own eyes, yeah dawg you're going pro after this season." Trey said.

"Thanks, that's the goal, but let's head home. I'm about to shower and want to order that pizza you ordered before." I said.

"Yeah, I can order that and it's your turn to pay soccer money. Haha, Oh yeah, I see you're a fast man. You got track speed, that's for sure. Speaking of track speed, one of the guys who ran track for the school wanted to talk to you. He was watching for a little bit too. I see him at the gym sometimes." Trey said.

"Sure, I don't mind having that convo with him." I said.

We started walking home and I checked my phone as I saw I had a text from Jessica, asking me what I was doing tonight. I texted back and told her I just got done playing soccer and about to shower and eat. I got a text from Star too, saying, "I hope to see you tomorrow at the bench party. Trey got the details already." She texted with a smiley face.

"Yes, I'll definitely be there for sure, beautiful." I texted her.

"Cool, I'll see you then,and you better know how to play volleyball too. We're having a tournament." She texted with a smile on her face.

Trey and I kept walking and made it home to our apartment. Trey ordered pizza as I gave him the money to pay for it. I went into my room, took my clothes off and put my dirty clothes in the dirty clothes basket and went to take a shower. When I was in the shower, I saw that my balls and dick area hair was getting long, so I opened the shaver pack I had on top of the toilet that was already here. I opened it and put soap on my balls and dick area as I shaved it to where it wasn't any hair anymore. My balls were smooth like eggs. After I showered, I dried myself off and turned on ESPN to watch soccer games. I saw that Jamaica were playing and my eyes were glued to the TV while putting cocoa butter on my skin. They were losing to Mexico. I was picturing myself on the team, making goals and hearing my country yell my name. I got a text from Jessica saying,

"I need to give you your healing cream. I forgot to give it to you. If you're not doing anything, you should come by and pick it up and chill with me for a little bit." Jessica texted.

I wanted to come over so I texted her.

"What is your address? I can see if I can get a ride if you're not far from campus. I would love to be your company." I texted.

I finished watching Jamaican soccer. I then heard a girl's voice in the living room as I cracked the door to see and it was a beautiful dark skin girl. She was a BBW on the size tip, but she didn't have a stomach, just a lot of booty and breasts. She also had long straight hair. She was wearing black leggings and a black and pink BBG shirt with the long finger nails to match. I saw Trey hugging her from behind and smacking her ass, telling her to get in his room. I just knew he was going to enjoy that nice body of hers.

Beep, I saw I got a text from Jessica saying that she's not far from campus and her house is actually close by and if I needed a ride, she would pick me up." I then texted her,

"Sure." And, gave her my address.

I went and got dressed. I put a white V neck on and put on these Grey sweat shorts I got from the mall. They were Nike shorts. I put socks on and my white Nike's. I also put on my Jamaican gold necklace and spray some cologne on me, then put on Irish spring deodorant. I brushed my teeth and washed my mouth out as well. I sat and waited as I kept watching the game. While watching the game, I heard moaning coming out the living room.

"Yes Trey!!!! Please go faster Daddy!"

I looked out the living room and I heard the back shaking. I started thinking, "Damn, this guy is putting in work" while laughing to myself. I then got a text from Jessica saying,

"I'm here."

I got hard because I knew I was going to have her body tonight. I texted her back.

"Coming right now."

I grabbed a few condoms and left my apartment. I looked over the balcony and saw a pink Range Rover, so I went down stairs and saw it was her. I remember her saying she had one. I walked up and went inside. She was playing Megan Thee Stallion, "Big Ole Freak" song.

"Hey you, and mmmm you smell good. I love a man that wears cologne and dresses nice too. It's a turn on." Jessica said while looking me up and down.

"Why, thank you. You smell good and look very nice yourself."

She was wearing booty shorts and her thighs were thick. She was wearing a black and pink BBG shirt.

"I see you're wearing that BBG shirt. I actually have been seeing women wear shirts. I'm happy for him that people are wearing his brand he designed." I said to her.

"Yes, I love it and I support people's dreams, plus I have a Big Booty. Don't you think so?" Jessica asked in a sexy funny voice.

"Yes, you do. Let me stop looking before I get in trouble." I said while I kept looking.

She smiled and pulled out of my apartment complex. We are heading to her place.

"So, is your mom white or black.?" I asked.

"My parents are black. Well, my mom is half white I just came out mixed looking because of her. My grandma, who is white was actually an amazing woman. I would spend weekends with her to hide from my parents with their super religious ass rules. She would let me do what I want, even bring my friends over. Boy, I miss her." Jessica said in a caring voice.

"I'm sorry for your loss. How did she pass away?" I asked.

"Well, she lived a full life. She was 95 when she passed away, just by old age got to her, you know. But we are here. This is my place." Jessica said

I look out the window. It was a normal sized house and the lights were on. We pulled up in her driveway. Then we got out of the car. I got a text from Trey, saying the pizza just got here. I started saying to myself, "damn it!!!" I texted him back saying, "I'll get it later." We then walked in her house. I looked around and it was very nice and clean. She had black a pink theme with her furniture. I also smelled food, too.

"I see that you love pink and black a lot and I smell that you cooked." I said while I kept looking around.

"Yes, my favorite colors, and yes, I did cook. I made steak and chicken tacos. Would you love some?" Jessica asked with a smile.

"Of course. I can eat right now." I said.

She walked me in the kitchen and started making me a plate. I sat down.

"Would you like a Powerade or soda"? Jessica asked while going into the refrigerator.

"Yes, a Powerade will be good." I said.

She made a plate. It was a chicken taco and a steak taco with brown rice on the side. She handed me salsa sauce, sour cream, chopped lettuce, cheese and chopped tomatoes. The food looked great and I started eating.

"Wow!! This is good. I see you can cook. I see why you're healthy now." I said with a smile while looking at her big booty.

"Yes, I love to cook and I love to feed a man too that loves to eat my cooking. Oh yeah, one of my friends saw you playing soccer and she said you were pretty good. She was out there with her man watching him play." Jessica said.

"Yeah it was packed out there. I'm happy she spoke well of me." I said while finishing eating.

"She said her boyfriend's teammates on their way home

were hating on you, talking shit, saying you think you're the shit, but I heard you blew them out. They didn't even score and you scored most of the points." Jessica said.

"Yeah. Haters will hate. Every great man has people who don't like him. I mean, look what happened to Jesus so I'm not surprised." I said while looking into her eyes.

"Yeah, you're right. You got some religion in you, looking at me with them green ass eyes." Jessica said while leaning over the kitchen table, talking to me.

I kept looking at her ass. It was just sitting up just right, plus she was beautiful as if Alica Keys had a young sister.

"I believe in a higher power, Alica Keys." I said while looking at her to see what she would say.

"You got jokes I see, that's funny. People call me that all the time in the ATL." Jessica said.

"You do favor her A lot. I love that Diary song. "I won't tell your secrets, your secrets are safe with meeeeeeeeeeee." I sang to Jessica while smiling.

"Damn, you sing too huh!! That actually sounds pretty good. Let me find out God made you special, special." Jessica said with a surprised look on her face.

"Yeah, I don't sing much, but hey, if soccer doesn't work out, maybe I'll join the music business, haha." I said with a laugh.

"With them white teeth and that smile, plus how nice you look, you'll do well in whatever you do in life, but here, let me get your healing cream from my room." Jessica said while walking to her room.

I watched her when she went into the room. Then I went inside my shorts to tuck my dick my away because I've pretty much been on hard the whole conversation. She came with the cream.

"Here you go, but let me rub some on your tattoo. Take your shirt off please." Jessica said, while holding the cream in her hand.

I took my shirt off and she started rubbing it on my body. Her hands felt good.

"So do you workout?" I asked.

"I do it when I can. It might be two to three times a week. Back when I was a stripper, I used to be in the gym 5 times a week. I even would drink protein shakes too. You gotta have upper body strength and endurance to dance, plus dancing is a workout itself, so I was in the best shape in my life back then. When I started tattooing full time and opened up my own business, I fell off." Jessica said while rubbing cream on my skin still.

"I can tell. Your arms are strong and your lower body is too. Like your butt is big and firm. You should dance for me." I said while looking.

"I can show you a little something. Here, sit on this chair." Jessica said.

I sat on the chair and she walked to her iPhone to connect it to the speaker as she turned the music on, playing the song, "Bandz A Make Her Dance." She started dancing and shaking her ass real fast. Then she put her ass on my lap and started shaking it on me. Out of nowhere, she pulled her shorts down and started making her ass clap. It was so loud, it sounded like I was clapping my hands together. Once I saw her ass cheeks and I heard the ass clap sound, then I got hard. My dick was poking out of my shorts.

"Looks like you're on hard. I see you must like the ass clap move huh." Jessica said while looking back at her ass on me.

"Yes, I do a lot." I said.

" You're an ass guy, huh?" Jessica asked.

"Yes, I am. I might have an ass fetish," I said,

"Mmmm, get up, come with me." Jessica said.

She took me to the living room, told me to sit on the floor and put my back against the couch.

"I want you to jack off while I'm shaking my ass on your face, and don't play dumb. I have been catching you looking at my ass and been seeing that big dick on hard since you've been here, my Jamaican friend." Jessica said with a smile

"You got me. Guilty as charged" I said.

"Well, whip it out. Hold up, I don't want you cumming all over my carpet." Jessica said while walking in the kitchen.

She gave me a few wet whips.

"There. Use that to catch all that nuts you about to bust out." She said while handing me the wet whips while pulling her pants down.

I whipped my dick out, started jacking off and she started shaking her big booty on my face. It felt like I was getting slapped by water balloons. Then she started making that ass clap sound again on my face. I started jacking off faster.

"Can I please put the tip of my dick between your ass cheeks while you clap your ass?" I asked in a kind way.

"Sure, but you're not getting pussy tonight. You will in due time if you play your cards right handsome." Jessica said while still shaking her ass.

I then stood up and put the tip of my dick between her ass cheeks and she started clapping her ass. It felt like my dick was getting a massage.

"You like that?" Jessica asked.

"Mmmmm, yes I do." I moaned.

She went faster with the ass clapping on my dick.

"I'm about to cum hard." I said.

"Go Head, baby. Please cum hard for me." Jessica said in a sexy voice.

I started cumming. Took my dick out and came on the wet whips.

"Damn, good shit. Thanks for not cumming on my ass cheeks, but next time, you can come inside my ass or my ass cheeks." Jessica said in a sexy voice, while pulling her shorts back up.

"Damn, you like anal?" I asked.

"I love anal, it feels great to me." Jessica said.

"Wow, that's sexy. I have never done it before. I mean, I'm down to try it." I said while finishing cleaning off the nut on my dick.

"Well, I can be your first next time. Here, let me take your sexy ass back home. It's getting late and I have to fly to Memphis tomorrow to do some tattoos on this rap group and some NFL players that play for the Titans. I'm going to be there for a week." Jessica said.

"Wow, you must be getting some good money to fly there." I said while putting my pants up and throwing away the wet whips.

"Yes, I will make 7,500 dollars while I'm there. They're paying for my room and they're flying out there too." Jessica said.

"Damn, that's amazing. Living the American dream. I love it. Your parents threw you out of the house and now you have your own house with a successful business. It's just motivation for me. I'm happy to know such a woman like you." I said.

"Yeah, it does feel good to be the boss haha, but I know you'll be here soon. I saw them nice soccer contracts. I looked it up and one player out of college got a $500,000 signing bonus with a 3 year 5 million deal, plus sponsors going to come with deals too. So trust and believe that your time will come soon. I will come to your house so you can cook dinner for me." Jessica said.

"Thanks, I needed to hear that beautiful." I said.

We then left her house and got in her Range Rover. She then dropped me off back in my apartment.

"Have a good night, Eason. I enjoyed your company handsome." Jessica said.

"I did too. Have a safe trip. Text me when you make it to Memphis to let me know that you're safe." I said while getting out of the car.

"Awww, aren't you the sweetest. I'll make sure I will and here's your cream. Don't forget to use it." Jessica said while handing me the cream.

Jessica left and I waved her goodbye. I went up the stairs to my apartment. I walked in while Trey was sitting on the couch, watching TV.

"Hey, what's up dawg. Your pizza is in the oven." Trey said.

"I'm going to put it in the Fridge. What show are you watching?" I asked.

"The show is called, "Power." It's produced by 50 cent. I'm on the last season." Trey said.

"I heard of it, I just never watched it. I heard it's good. I need to watch it." I said while walking to the oven and putting the pizza in the fridge.

"Yeah, people have been going on social media about the Trey Songz intro part, but I'm a Trey Songz's fan so it is what it is with me. Shit is crazy though. You must have eaten already with a chick or something." Trey said.

"Yeah, I ate tacos with Jessica." I said.

"Jessica from the tattoo shop?" Trey said while looking at me to see what I will say.

"Yes I did, she was wearing your BBG shirt that you gave her." I said.

"That's what's up. She's supporting the brand, so you went to her house? And what did y'all do?" Trey asked.

"We just ate tacos and had a good convo. She's actually going to Memphis to do tattoos for NFL players and rappers. They're even flying her out there." I said.

"She's getting that money. She is her own boss. That shit is smooth. That's going to be me pretty soon, traveling all over and getting paid for it, too." Trey said.

"Yeah, so I saw a woman in here earlier. Sounds like y'all was having a good time, haha." I said with a laugh.

"Hahaha, yeah. That's one of my friends. She is supporting my brand." Trey said while laughing.

"Yeah, you have a lot of friends that's women I see, haha. To be honest, you never talk about your friends from home, like your male friends." I said.

"Yeah, Because I cut them all off." Trey said.

"Why did you do that?" I said while sitting on the lazy boy across from him.

"They are not doing anything with their life, man. Some of them became coke heads, some became alcoholics and the others were just hating ass bitch ass niggas, to be honest. I used to have a best friend. My right hand man, he was my dawg man, but over the years, he just got worse." Trey said.

"What do you mean?" I asked.

"He got worse. He didn't want to support my dreams, just talked down about my dreams because people were fucking with my dreams, you know. Like I remember I was signed to a publishing company because I'm a good writer also. The bitch nigga told me to stop doing it and that shit isn't going to get any where. I remember I was at a barber shop right, and he was down talking to me about my publishing company and me calling it fake, just on some hating ass shit. My dumb ass listened to him and quit the publishing company because I wasn't used to all this hate coming from someone close. Then I remember another time when I started BBG. He was hating. He wouldn't support the shit at all, but when someone talks bad about my brand, he would be quick to tell me the negative shit then the positive. Shit is crazy, man. I just outgrew the niggas I used to chill with back then. Ain't no beef or nothing. I just don't rock with them because I know when the big money come in, they are going to start hating on me hard and I don't want to be around that type of energy, you know." Trey said.

"Damn, sounds like people you don't need around you at all while you are doing this good." I said.

"Yes, my right hand became my left hand and started to envy me over the years. When we used to work at this gas station together and became roommates, he started seeing all the women come in my room, not his. That shit got to him when women started wearing my BBG brand. That shit got to him. He became negative. I cut the hoe ass nigga off. He went to social media like a bitch. Like an emotional female and started down talking to me about my BBG brand and shit. That happened years ago. It's like damn, you must have felt like this for a long time. I mean, it's my fault though women told me about him and I didn't listen. That's why I keep a lot of women around me. They are more trustworthy, you know." Trey said.

"Well, you don't have to worry about me turning on you, plus I love your BBG brand. I think it's genius, you know." I said.

"I appreciate that, for real. Keep the real ones around you that want to see you grow like my mans G herbo said.

Used to wonder, will I ever count a million or obtain 100?
And every time when I went broke, I still remained 100.
Supported niggas doing good, I never changed or nothing.
But why do they hate on me? Tried to close the gate on

me.

"Why do niggas wanna throw they extra dead weight on me" Trey rapped.

"Damn, that's deep. Sounds like these guys hurt you, man. Some people are just here for seasons in your life. When their time is up, it's up. Trust me, you got me and you're going to have new dawgs who see your vision and want to see you win the future with BBG." I said while giving him a hand shake and getting up to get ready for bed.

"Thanks dawg, you're right. The future is BBG; it's just sad how my old friends have all this talent and they're just letting it go to waste. That shit hurt dawg. Two of them can be in the NFL or playing football in Canada somewhere. The other is a people person. He can easily become a party promoter and get paid for it, but they rather down talk me dawg and hate while wasting their talents. God bless them. It's getting late, it's about 1 pm. It's time for me to go to bed. When we get up, I plan on going to Walmart to get swimming trunks, then after that, we are going to hit the road to Chicago to see what this beach party is talking about." Trey said.

"Alright, I'll set my alarm at 9am. I'll be up and ready." I said while walking in my room.

"Cool. Night, dawg." Trey said while walking in his room.

I went in my room got my clothes together that I was going to wear tomorrow. I checked the weather and it was going to be 85 degrees and sunny, so I got a white tank top and my Jamaican colored shorts. I went to brush my teeth, wash my mouth out and set my alarm for 9am. I then went to bed.

CHAPTER 6

I woke up at 8:55 am. I looked outside my window. It was sunny out and I turned the TV on to watch ESPN and Jamaica lost to Mexico: 4 to 2. I said to myself, "We should have beat them." I got up got naked and turned the shower on. Started brushing my teeth and washed my mouth out. I took a shower and I saw that it was hard. I closed my eyes and picture myself having sex with Jessica and I started jacking off in the shower. I imagined myself eating her pussy from the back while I massaged her ass cheeks. Then, I came all over the shower floor. My nut went down the drain as I finished washing my body. I was finished with my shower. I dried off, rubbed cocoa butter on my skin and got dressed. I put on my Jamaica color snap back with my earrings, my Jamaica gold necklace, tank top, Jamaica color shorts socks with Jamaica color Nike's. I sprayed cologne on, opened my dresser and took 100 dollars out of spending money. I can hear Trey in the living. I opened the door and saw that Trey was dressed. I'm ready as well. He was wearing a white and red BBG tank top. It looked like he got a fresh cut too because his waves were on swim mode and had a nice lining.

"Good, I see you're ready. I'm about to go grab a breakfast sandwich and we can head out. I thought I needed swim trunks, but I found my old ones. I don't really plan on swimming anyway." Trey said.

Yeah, me either, but I'm ready to go and where are we getting breakfast?" I asked because I was hungry too.

"McDonald's. I love their bagel breakfast sandwich." Trey said.

"Alright, I want one too. Hold up, let me go to my room." I said.

I checked my phone and got a text from Kendra, Lisa, Nisha and Jessica, basically saying good morning to me with smiling faces. Jessica texted me, saying she made it to Memphis. I texted everyone back and told Jessica good and I want another tattoo when you get back, beautiful. Trey and I left our apartment. It was hot and sunny outside. We got inside his Jeep and went to get breakfast. We pulled up to McDonald's and got bagel breakfast sandwiches with orange juice, then he went to the gas station and started to head to Chicago. I was excited because I always wanted to know what Chicago was like. I got a text from Star.

"Good morning, sexy. I hope you and Trey are on y'all way." She texted with a smiley face.

"Yes, we're actually on the road now, chocolate star." I texted with a smile.

"Well, we are on our way to Chicago. About to pop in some Chicago music." Trey said while driving and going through his iPhone.

He started playing Chief Keef's first album 'Finally Rich.' After driving for a while, he turned down the music.

"So, I looked into how much land costs in Jamaica and it doesn't cost much. It's a great idea that you want to get into that business. People all over the world will want to buy from you." Trey said.

"Yes, then I can bring a lot of money in my community. I will build homes across my community. I don't need a lot of money to live life. I don't need 100 million dollars just to be sitting in my bank account. I don't need 5 or more cars. That's why black athletes go broke. They try to live this rich lifestyle, trying to impress people who don't give a fuck about them. Whatever soccer gives me, I will buy land to build my home. A nice home. I don't need houses all over and I don't want to spend thousands of dollars on clothes alone. That's foolish to me, me giving back to my community is rich to me. A lot of us have been poor for way too long. I will change that. I got a lot of ideas, a lot of people outside Jamaica are coming from China and other places, using us and sucking us dry. I will change that. They are buying up our land and building hotels, just making sure their people are good, not Jamaica's." I said with passion.

"Wow!! Man, that's a deep sound. Like you should be a part of your community council. Be a part of the politics of things that will help the community a lot as well. Sorry that's going on in Jamaica. I never knew that, but getting into politics will help your country, not just money, you know." Trey said in a caring voice.

"Yeah, maybe I should, maybe I should."

I loved the idea Trey told me about joining politics. That made me think about signing up for a politics class as well this fall. I then fell asleep.

"Wake Up dawg. We made it to Chicago. I don't want you to kiss the Skyscrapers and the Sears tower." Trey said.

I started waking up and I saw skyscrapers and the Sears tower. I had never seen such a tall building before in my life. The traffic was super busy. It was exciting to me.

"That place right there is called Harold's chicken. We're going to have to eat there sometime. You will love it. Something about that sauce. We have great soul food restaurants too. And another thing about Chicago: It's always something to do here, not like our own small college town where we live." Trey said with excitement.

He kept showing and pointing at different places in Chicago, then we made it. I can see the sand on the beach with hundreds of people there.

"Looks like we made it here. Let's find a parking spot. I can see the Alpha girls. They're by the Volleyball net." Trey said.

We found a parking spot. We stepped out of the Jeep. It was nice and hot, so I took my tank top off and rub healing cream all over my tattoo and put my phone and wallet under the Jeep seat. I looked and saw the alpha girls too, with a lot of other girls and guys. The music was loud too.

"Damn, they have a DJ out there too. I was wondering where that music was coming from." Trey said while looking around.

"Yeah, I'm loving the vibe out here. This reminds me of Jamaica, seeing this many people on a beach, but our water is much more clear." I said.

"Yeah, but y'all have sharks, we don't haha! But, let's go check out the party they're dancing at." Trey said.

We walked over to the Alpha girls and I saw Star.

"What in the chocolate God? Who is that? Damn, he is beautiful." An Alpha girl said.

"His name is Eason. He moved here from Jamaica." Star said while giving me a hug.

"I love your hair. I see you got your dreads braided and damn you got a new tattoo too? Man, this is really nice." Star said while looking at my tattoo.

"Thanks, I plan on getting more." I said.

Star was looking good. She was wearing a red two piece swimsuit. Everything on her looked good. I can see she even had abs too.

"Y'all want something to eat? We got drinks too." Star said.

"No, I'm alright right now. I see there's a lot of y'all here."
I said while looking around.

"So who is this dark chocolate handsome brother? They
just told me you're from Jamaica." An Alpha girl said.

"Yes, I am. Nice to meet you. What's your name?" I asked.

"Thirsty Hoe." Star whispered under her breath.

"My name is Amber. I see you came here with the other
handsome brother too, but I prefer tall, dark and handsome. So
are you single Mr. Jamaican man, with green eyes?" Amber
asked.

"Amber, I need your help over here. Hurry up." A guy said.

"I'll be right back." Amber said with a smile.

Amber then walked off.

"I can't stand her messy thirsty ass. She needs to take her
pale skin ass on." Star said.

"She isn't your friend?" I asked.

"Hell naw. She's trying to be an Alpha girl like me. She
thinks because she's light skin and pretty, she can pull any guy
she wants. She says it all the time, plus when they were talking
about you, about that video, she asked questions about you." Star
said in an upset voice.

"Well, she isn't my type. You're my type." I said while
looking in her eyes.

I can tell what I said made Star feel good and she started
to smile.

"Well, come over here. I want you to meet everybody." Star said while we walked over to her friends.

"Hey, everyone. This is Eason. He moved here from Jamaica. He's playing soccer at ISU this season."

"This is the strong Jamaican man that was lifting those heavy weights in that video." An Alpha girl said.

"Yes, that's him." Star said.

"Your ass is strong boy. Well, you can play on my team. We're about to play Volleyball now anyway." An Alpha girl said while looking me up and down.

I saw Nicki, Tara and Judy, the Alpha girls we ate at the pancake house with.

"He can dance too. He was doing some Jamaican stroll at the club." Nicki said.

"Yeah, he needs to teach us so us Alpha girls can use that stroll." Judy said.

Then, a guy with his friends walked up and one of them went to talk to Star, "Hey Star, it's been awhile since I've seen you." the guy said.

Everybody started looking and the whole vibe just changed as Trey came up to me.

"I remember these niggas. Star and I went to Jacksonville college with them. They were on some gang banging shit. They got kicked out for stealing. That one is talking, his name is

Anthony." Trey said to me in a low voice.

"What y'all doing? About to play volleyball? We're down to play too." Anthony said.

Anthony and his three friends just looked like trouble and felt like trouble. They had tattoos on their face and neck.

"Yeah, y'all can play with us." Judy said.

We picked teams up and started the tournament. Star, Nicki, Judy, Trey and Amber were on my team against the other alpha girls and their friends. We won our first game and we waited for the other two teams to play.

"Hey, is your name Trey?" A random girl asked.

"Yes, my name is Trey. What's your name?" Trey asked.

"My name is Kenisha. So you're the one that owns that BBG Brand, right?" Kenisha asked.

"Yes, you want a shirt? I got a few of them in the back." Trey said with a smile.

"Sure, but I wanted to talk business with you. I am opening a club in Houston TX. It opens in November. I would love to have a BBG night. Star told me about your BBG goals and I love the ideas, plus I know other club owners who would love to meet with you as well." Kenisha said with a smile.

"OMG, you foreal!!" Trey said while his eyes started to water.

"Yes, I'm foreal. My club is called "Sexy Nights" and I want your brand in my club. I'm going to have NFL players, NBA players and rappers come to my opening night. I know people and I'm a fan of your brand. I will pay you as well and we can get a contract together too." Kenisha said.

"Damn, my dreams are coming true. Here, come with me. I'm getting you some of my shirts." Trey said with a big happy smile on his face.

I was happy for Trey that his dreams were about to come true. He went through a lot for his brand BBG, but it was pretty chill. I was drinking beer and eating BBQ ribs, talking to Star and the alpha girls about Jamaica and asking them questions about America. They were beautiful women with great conversation.

"Looks like we're up next." Star said.

So my team went to the sand to play. We were playing against Anthony and his friends. He even had two girls on his team that weren't alpha girls.

"Welp, y'all about to lose. This is easy money." Anthony said.

"Naw, y'all are about to lose." Star said.

I served the volleyball and hit the ball over the net. The other team hit the ball over, Trey then power slammed the ball and he scored us a point as we started celebrating.

"That lucky ass shit. Y'all act like y'all won a championship." One of Anthony's guys said.

"We are going to beat y'all." Nicki said.

We kept going back and forth. We were playing to see

who got to 10 first for the championship round, both teams then got up to 9 each. It was my serve again. I hit the ball over, they hit back then I jumped up really high, hit a power slam and scored the winner point. We celebrated again.

"Damn Dawg, you got up there. I'm pretty sure you can dunk if you wanted to." Trey said with a surprised face.

"It doesn't matter. We're still getting money though. Y'all broke ass college kids stick to eating noodles." Anthony said.

"Broke!!! Nigga get your ugly ass out of here. Y'all just mad y'all lost. That's why your dumb ass got kicked out of school we heard." Nicki said while everybody laughed.

"Bitch!!!!" Anthony went over and punched Nicki in the face.

"What the fuck, you're punching on females because she called your retarded ass out." Trey then ran up and punched Anthony in his face.

Then his friends came to fight Trey. I ran up and started punching and body slamming niggas. The alpha girls came up to the fight too to fight the niggas. They can brawl. Trey grabbed a beach chair. I picked up Anthony and body slammed him like a rag doll and Trey hit him with the beach chair. We were beating their ass. Two of them and more of his Antoney friends came out of nowhere. There were 5 more. Two of them tried to jump me, but I punched one and hit him so hard that he went to sleep. The other one, I picked him up and body slammed him. The bawl lasted about 3 mins, then we saw cops running to us! Trey was on top of one, beating his ass. I grabbed him and told him cops were running to us and we needed to leave. Everybody started running, even the Alpha girls. We all ran to our cars. Trey and I out ran everybody and made it to the Jeep.

"Let's get the fuck out of here before cop cars get here." Trey said while starting the car up.

We got pulled out of the lot and got in the street as Trey got us out of there.

"Damn, that was a close one! Them bitch ass niggas was on some hating shit! He bogus ass hell for punching Nicki like that. I had to punch him. Good shit for running up on them other niggas." Trey said while driving and catching his breath.

"Yeah, I had to join in. I couldn't let you have all the fun yourself." I said while catching my breath and looking around.

"Hahaha, bro we were on some WWE shit. I grabbed the motherfucking chair because I was going to hit Anthony dumb ass with it and your Jamaican ass grabbed him and slammed on the ground. And, I hit him with that motherfucker ahahaha!" Trey said while laughing and driving.

"Hahaha, I was watching you and I knew you wanted to hit him with the chair, so I said fuck it. Let me help my dawg so I slammed him. You can hit him, Hahaha." I laughed while giving him a handshake.

"Bro, I'm dead haha, but the Alpha girls weren't going

fam. They were beating niggas asses and they beat them ugly ass hoes up too. Shit was too crazy, but other than that, that party was fun and I love the good news I got too. I got Kenisha's number, her chocolate ass is too sexy." Trey said while driving.

"Yeah, I'm very happy for you, plus she has connections. She said when everything goes well for you, you're going to be moving to Huston?" I asked.

"Hell yeah dawg. I told you football isn't my dream. This BBG shit is. After this football season, I'm moving to Huston. If the money looks right and she's very serious and the contract looks good, I'm gone. I need to thank Star for helping me out." Trey said.

"Yeah, Matter of fact, let me see if they made it out ok. I'm going to call her." I said.

"They made it out ok, because when we made it, the alpha girls were right behind us." Trey said.

I started calling Star.

"Hello, are you ok?" I asked Star while putting the phone on the speaking phone so that Trey could hear.

"Yes, we made it out of that jam. We made it out safely. Thanks for checking on us. Them niggas were hating on us hard and they bogus for putting they hands on Nicki." Star said on speaker phone.

"Hell yeah. They were hating. That's why they got their ass beat." Trey said.

"Haha, Thank y'all for helping us, we're going to Nicki house for a bit to chill out, but we'll talk to y'all later. We should be back at ISU tonight if y'all not doing nothing, y'all can come over to play cards and drink with us." Star said on the speaker phone.

"Sure, I'm down for that." I said.

"Yes, I'm down for that too. I'll see y'all later on." Trey said.

"Alright, see y'all later." Star said while hanging up.

"Them girls are smart. Going back home to chill, not going to the club in the city." Trey said.

"Why do you say that?" I asked while looking at my phone.

"Because Niggas from Chicago be hating dawg. They got they ass whooped and sometimes niggas, can't take an ass beating, so if anything, them niggas will watch them Alpha girls social media or mines to see where we be at. If we go to any clubs, they be there to fight again with more niggas or shoot at us. I've seen this many times. That's why I'm driving straight home because we got shit to lose. They don't, you know. That's why I moved out of the city. The Alpha girls will tell you the same too." Trey said while driving on the highway.

"Wow, that's crazy. It does make sense" I said.

I looked at my phone and I had texts from Kendra, Lisa and Jessica saying that they liked my soccer video of me playing, and a lot of people are sharing it all over social media.

"I guess a video of me playing soccer from last night went viral. I didn't know people were taking a video of me. I just got words from a few of my lady friends." I said with a surprised tone.

"Yeah dawg, there were a lot of people there recording their games, plus that Crazy ass bicycle kick was something crazy like the movies to be honest." Trey said while driving.

I saw I had a missed call and a voicemail was left. I went to play the voicemail on speaker so I can hear the phone better.

"Hey, how are you doing, Eason? My name is Kevin Mitchell and I am a Sports Agent. I know a few teams that have interest in you. I know you have a season to finish, but I've seen the money they are willing to give you. I heard you want to be one and done. Well, after watching your high school highlights and the video that went viral of you playing, these teams love your speed and your amazing ball handling. To be honest, we are surprised you didn't go pro after high school, but hey, I'm here to help you and show you the promise land to a lot of money. Call me when you get a chance, please. This is my number. Have a great day bud." The voicemail said.

Trey and I then looked at each other speechless. We had nothing to say.

To Be Continued

Made in the USA
Monee, IL
08 August 2023

40649718R00104